If Not, Wat Will?

Steve Gooch

written in conjunction with Guy Sprung
and The Half Moon

Pluto Press

First published 1975 by
Pluto Press Limited,
Unit 10, Spencer Court,
7 Chalcot Road,
London NW1 8LH.

ISBN 0 902818 63 5

Design by Richard Hollis, GrR

Printed photolitho in Great Britain
by Ebenezer Baylis and Son Ltd.,
The Trinity Press, Worcester, and London

Will Wat, If Not, What Will?

First performed at
The Half Moon Theatre Club on
Friday, 27 May 1972
with the following cast:

John Ball	Maurice Colbourne
Wat Tyler	Michael Irving
Richard II	Mary Sheen
Christopher Southíen	Ruth Seglow
Thomas Baker	Sarah Dearsley
William Walworth	Robin Culver
Salisbury	David Stockton
Jack Straw	Peter Wickham
Sudbury	Yvonne Gilan
Hales	Terence Dougherty

Directed by Guy Sprung
Designed by Fay Barratt
Music by Robin Marsden

Will Wat,

Writer's Note

When we did this show at The Half Moon we only had
10 actors, which meant the doubling was ridiculous. But that
didn't matter. We weren't presenting a formal theatrical
representation of The Peasants' Revolt — a 'play' — rather
it was these 10 actors telling and showing the audience what
happened to the peasants and artisans in 1381. And that
meant a lot of hard work for them, both in rehearsal and
performance. The actors wore a basic peasant costume over
which they slung cloaks and hats for middle-class characters,
cassocks and mitres for clergy, bits of armour for soldiers,
and so on. Whatever they had time to grab or get into
between scenes.

We played with the audience on three sides and had
gangways leading into the three blocks. The acting area was
laid with thick, rough wooden joists and the interior of the
Half Moon was covered with beams and mud-painted hessian.
Upstage left was the musical apparatus corner. We had a
2 cwt anvil, two out-of-tune church bells, a 98 gallon
hogshead drum, a smaller drum also made from a barrel, a
trombone, a recorder and a jaw harp. Upstage right was a
small raised area which we used for indoor scenes. This was
confined in height by the heavy beams which supported the
balcony or gallery. The balcony was used for Court scenes
and was hung with purple drapes to provide a shallow
proscenium acting area. At the back of the auditorium was a
huge reproduction of the Westminster Abbey portrait of
Richard the Second, glaring down on the audience.

The script was, of course, written expressly for the Half
Moon auditorium, but the physical specifications are not as
important as the way in which the material is played. It
must be informal. The actors must contact their audience,
though it is no good 'playing' this. They should be like
people getting up at a family party and doing their turn.
At the Half Moon they didn't have to play this, it happened
naturally.

What's written here is almost exactly what was performed at
The Half Moon. I've made a few alterations, cleaned up a
few lines, put in a few explanations and changed the bits
that made me wince the most. In our version we took an
interval after the Northampton Parliament scene. This
represented a break between the 'causes' of the revolt and
the more documentary scenes showing its progression. This
meant we had a first half of about an hour and a second
half of ninety minutes. We didn't do the Main Road from
Canterbury to London scene and the Norwich scene, but I've
included them here. In a version which included these scenes

— and perhaps excluded others — it might be better to take the break after John Ball's speech at Maidstone. Otherwise the most crucial changes have been to the first Blackheath scene, the Smithfield scene and the Garter Lane scenes, which we never really worked out satisfactorily in rehearsal. I hope this script as it stands now makes sense to any reader who didn't see the production.

Finally, in our production at The Half Moon we wanted to avoid 'Mummerset' acting as far as possible and tried to evolve a kind of medieval rural dialect of our own, which would show something of the more physical nature of language in those days. By contrast we thought of a nasal, frenchified accent for the nobility, but straight 'posh' worked very well for them. At all events there is no point, if one is trying to show what the history books usually leave out, in reproducing the peasants and labourers of bad Shakespeare productions.

[**A Solitary Actor** comes into the acting area. He sings:]

'Man beware and don't hold back
Think upon the block and on the axe
The axe was sharp, the block was hard
In the fourth year of King Richard.'

[**An Actor** dressed as a peasant comes on, pushing a heavy
medieval cart loaded with bales of wool, shepherds' tools,
etc. He is followed by **A Group of Actors** dressed likewise.
Someone announces:]

England, 1340: Open Country

[**The Actors** are a group of shepherds. They work for a
while, silent. **Roger** comes on.]

Roger:	Still at it, brothers?
Young Shepherd:	Look who's here.
1 Shepherd:	We shorn fifty sheep this morning, Roger.
Young Shepherd:	You come back, then.
Roger:	Passing through. — What's this for?

[He picks up a pig's bladder from the cart.]

Roger:	Archery practice?
Young Shepherd:	Football's more fun. What good's a longbow to us?
Roger:	For fighting Frenchmen. If your lord calls you up.
2 Shepherd:	I ain't been ten miles out the vill, let alone over the sea. They want you to fight, let 'em teach you when you get there.
Roger:	You've got to look after yourself. Out in the wide world. To get what you want. A bow can come in handy these days. On your real enemies.
Old Shepherd:	We're happy as we are, Roger.
Roger:	Soldiers in the vill when I came up.
Old Shepherd:	They come through.
Roger:	Never used to. Nothing else's changed, though.
3 Shepherd:	I don't know.
Roger:	If it has, it's for the worse.
3 Shepherd:	No. We got our own barn now. Philip's bought himself a strip of land in the wastes. For the better, if anything.
Roger:	Well, you're older, aren't you.
3 Shepherd:	Eh?
Roger:	You come into the world naked. By the time you die, if there's no shirt on your back, you've wasted your time. Old Thomas dead?
1 Shepherd:	Yeh.
Roger:	Who got his sow?

1

Young Shepherd: I did.

2 Shepherd: 'Cept he ain't paid the fine on it.

Young Shepherd: I got till Easter!

Roger: Supposing you peg out? Your missus won't get it. Do you see what I mean? There's only so much to go round. You break your backs up here and you've got two pounds' worth of goods and a few pence in your pocket when you die.

2 Shepherd: Where'd you pinch your fancy jacket, then, Roger?

Roger: Watch it, serf!

2 Shepherd: Who you calling names?

Roger: Look at this. [He opens his jacket.] Mean anything?

2 Shepherd: No.

Roger: Personal insignia of Lord Percy. [He shows it round.] There's only him and John of Gaunt in the country's got them. I'm his steward. Ten pound fourteen a year.

Young Shepherd: Ten pound fourteen?

Roger: More'n you'd see in a lifetime. I told you to get out.

Young Shepherd: How'd you do it?

Roger: While you're stuck out here in this wilderness, trying to squeeze crops out of ground that's dead before you start, there's men in the towns and manors making fortunes. Out of this stuff. [He picks up some clippings.] It's like gold in Norwich. Bundle like that [he points] 's worth five shillings.

3 Shepherd: Five shillings?

2 Shepherd: That's more'n a week's wages for all of us.

1 Shepherd: How they do it, Roger?

Roger: There's no end of tricks. They buy up great quantities when it comes into market, then hold on to it. Over in Flanders the cloth trade's crying out for it. The weavers can't get enough. So up goes the price. When it's high enough, these fellas sell it for four, five times what they paid for it. King Edward was the first to catch on. Brought all these Flemings over to show our merchants how. He's made a fortune for his wars. Keeping Alice Perrers in jewels. Now everyone's caught on.

2 Shepherd: You an' all, Roger?

Roger: You got to have money to buy the wool in the first place. I ain't doing that well. Even so, you're supposed to pay my board and lodging in the vill tonight, you know that?

3 Shepherd: Board for you!

Young Shepherd: Shit!

Roger: I'm on my way down to London for Lord Percy. Even better clippings down there.

2 Shepherd: Don't tell us, the sheep are all golden.

2

Roger: There's no sheep in London. Just wool.

Old Shepherd: The Lord's my shepherd, Roger. That's what they teach. A father is a shepherd is a lord.

Roger: That means, you fleece the sheep and your lord fleeces you. A child is a sheep is a slave. And naughty children must be punished or they grow up evil. They teach you that too. Only look at me. I wasn't a good boy and I haven't done so bad.

1 Shepherd: We ain't got time to look at you. There's a hundred more sheep want shearing before dark.

[**Roger** gets up.]

Roger: I'll be staying down at Matt's. Call by this evening. I'll buy you a drink.

2 Shepherd: That's the least you can do, if we're paying your board.

[A **Sergeant-at-Arms** and A **Bailiff** come on.]

Sergeant: Lord Percy's steward?

Roger: That's right.

Sergeant: This man is a deserter from His Majesty's Army and a thief. Take him.

[Pause. No-one knows what to do.]

Sergeant: [To **Shepherds**.] You know he's a serf, don't you?

[**Roger** decides to run.]

Sergeant: Stop him !

[**One of the Shepherds** trips him.]

Roger: Cunt !

[**The Bailiff** and **The Sergeant** hold him.]

Bailiff: Had a feeling it was you, Roger [to **Sergeant**]. Ran away three years ago.

2 Shepherd: What he do, Gil?

Bailiff: Stole this jacket from a draper in Norwich. Been passing as a steward all over Suffolk, unsettling people. I knew the face and the coat didn't fit.

Sergeant: Come on.

[**The Bailiff, Roger** and **The Sergeant** go off. **The Young Shepherd** tries to stuff wool in his shirt.]

1 Shepherd: [Stopping him.] Don't learn, will you. If you took that all the way to market, you'd get twopence. That's a day's work for a day's money. Come on, let's get busy!

[The scene breaks. **A Knight in Armour** clatters in and orders **The Peasants,** who were **The Shepherds,** to lift him on his horse by means of a trapeze on a pulley. **The Horse** played by **Two Actors. Someone** announces:]

1345: King Edward the Third
attends a Jousting Match with his mistress
Alice Perrers

[**Edward III** appears on the balcony with his mistress **Alice Perrers.** She throws a favour to **The Knight.** They watch the jousting throughout the scene.]

Edward: They're not good, Alice.
Alice: That's hardly my fault, Edward.
Edward: Pick any ten Frenchmen and nine of them could run rings round this lot with one hand behind their back.
Alice: They're very young.
Edward: You would notice that. [He signals for the jousting to start
Alice: There's nothing else here for a woman to get excited about.

[**The Knight** on his **Horse** charges off, lance and all. There i a loud crash offstage.]

Edward: You're supposed to be blushing and swooning at their skill and bravery. Like in the romances.
Alice: They smell, Edward.
Edward: The trouble is, their fathers are too busy finding ways of not giving me money to teach them about fighting — or parfume
Alice: You're obsessed with your wretched army.
Edward: If it wasn't for the army, my dear, you wouldn't be wearing the latest French fashions.
Alice: Second hand. [She fingers her dress.]
Edward: My son brought that all the way from Amiens for you. The least you can do is look interested. I've got angry Scots to the North, belligerent Irish to the West, the Duke of Flander after our wool to the East, and the French demanding their wine trade back in the South, and you turn your nose up at what amounts to a training session.

[**Another Knight** comes on on his **Horse,** slightly bettered.

Alice: You're just turning out bullies.
Edward: An efficient fighting force. Better than the bunch of snotty peasants with plough handles we had before. I've got the Eyeties over a barrel with my army.
Alice: It doesn't even fit.
Edward: What?

Alice: The dress. I think it was cut for a hunchback midget.

Edward: You'll be giving the poor boy measurements next. At least he got the colour right.

Alice: Blue.

Edward: So?

Alice: I asked for turquoise.

Edward: The Black Prince is a soldier, not a draper!

Alice: Then it's time he learnt. Along with all your other little soldier boys. It's not the army that's making England rich, it's the wool trade, and you know it. Those Eyeties as you call them, in their lovely coats and cloaks, are financing your son's little jaunts abroad. They know how to make money. And if you didn't know how to take it from them, this island would be a desert and I'd be off home to France.

Edward: They may be smart, but we're catching on, don't worry.

[He signals for another charge.]

Alice: Twenty years after the rest of Europe, as always.

[**The Second Knight** charges off. Another crash. **Edward** and **Alice** wave. **Richard Lyons** comes on to the balcony.]

Edward: Oh my God. It's Dick Lyons. I wanted to avoid him.

Lyons: Your Majesty.

Edward: Dick.

Lyons: Ma'am.

Alice: Hello, Dick.

[Silence. They watch the jousting. **The First Knight** returns with bent lance.]

Alice: [Winking to **Lyons**.] How are things, Dick?

Lyons: [Smiling too broadly.] Very good, Ma'am.

Alice: [Nodding towards **Edward** — they are baiting him.] I'm glad to hear it.

[Silence. **Edward** stares fixedly at the jousting. He signals and **The First Knight** charges off again.]

Lyons: Perhaps Edward hasn't told you. We raised the price of wool from five pounds to nine pounds and it's turned out very well for us.

Alice: [Admiring.] Really?

Edward: [Looking straight ahead.] They held their stocks back, that's why.

Alice: Well there you are, Edward. Richard knows the market's more important than smelly soldiers, even if you don't.

5

Edward: Without my smelly soldiers, we'd be an Italian province and Richard Lyons would be a pauper.

Alice: But you can't say your leading citizens aren't smart, Edward

Edward: Too smart. All the money I make goes into the army and protects merchants like him so that they can make more money, which they keep for themselves.

Lyons: You haven't done badly out of us, Edward, in the past.

Edward: Not any more, though.

Lyons: We support you.

Edward: But you name the price.

Lyons: I think that's fair. After all, you don't really like foreigners, do you. You're in their debt as it is.

Edward: I brought the Italians over here to teach us the trade. Before they came, you didn't even know you were Englishmen. There was a big market for our wool in Flanders, and you were too thick to tap it.

Lyons: I think we've learned how to be Englishmen now, Edward.

Edward: Too bloody right you have! At least the Italians behave with respect while they're here. Anybody'd think you owned this country!

Lyons: We very nearly do.

Edward: So I suppose you want me to get rid of the Italians?

Lyons: Edward the First got rid of the Jews, didn't he? Ten thousand moneylenders drowned at sea as they were on their way out and the Eyeties on their way in.

Edward: I can't drown the Bardi and the Peruzzi. The Pope would execute me in person.

Lyons: I thought the Vatican disapproved of usury.

Edward: Not when it's getting its cut.

Lyons: So what, then?

Edward: You tell me.

Lyons: Tax them. It's more profitable. They've been importing false coinage, so get your own back. Have new coins struck. Let us take over the Customs and appoint one of us Mayor of the Wool Staple.

Edward: So you control it instead of me.

Lyons: Leaves you more time for this sort of thing. [Jousting — he gestures.]

Edward: Leaves you unchecked, more like.

Lyons: It's either us or the Italians. And we've got the Hansa towns on our side.

Edward: And they've got my crown.

Lyons: They said you'd pawned it to them. I told them I found that hard to believe.

Edward: 45,000 gold crowns if you must know. — What do I get out of this?

Lyons: Now the price is up from five pounds to nine pounds, we thought we'd subsidise you two pounds a sack.

Edward: Big of you. Who gets the other two pounds?

Lyons: That's our guarantee against your interfering with trade by any political means. No embargos, blocking or seizing merchant ships without compensation. We've got to be protected.

[**The First Knight** comes back. He holds **Alice's** favour up weakly towards the balcony, then falls flat on his back. **Edward** stands.]

Edward: You'll do.

Lyons: What does that mean?

Edward: These may be shit [the jousters] but at least my businessmen have grown up.

[They go off. **The Peasants** carry **The Knight** off. As they do, they sing 'Money, money':]

Money, money, now hey good day
Money, where hast thou been
Money, money, thou goest away
And wilt not bide with me.

The ploughman himself does dig and delve
In snow, frost and rain
Money to get with labour and sweat
But much pain and small gain.

Money, money etc.

Above all things thou art the King
And rul'st the world over all
Who lacketh thee all joy pardee
Must soon them from him fall.

Money, money etc.

[As they finish the song, **A Peasant** stumbles forward, collapses and dies. The others gather round him, inspect him, then carry him off. **Someone** announces:]

In 1348 the Black Death hit England. Carried by fleas on rats

[Three rats scuttle across the acting area. Screams from **The Peasants.**]

There were three different kinds of plague; bubonic plague, a long and painful death; pneumonic plague, a short and sudden death; and septicaemonic, spread by direct contagion between individuals. Together these three kinds of plague decimated nearly one third of the population.

[**The Peasants** begin to hand out undertakers' business card to every third member of the audience.]

However, as the plague thrived best in unhygienic conditions, the rich were less affected than the poor.

[**The Peasants** do not give cards to the smarter-looking members of the audience. **Richard Lyons,** who has come down from the balcony and has been listening with a worried frown, now smiles and shakes hands with the announcer, who announces:]

**1350: A Typical Knight
returns from the wars in France
and meets A Typical Bishop**

[**The Peasants** go off. **A Knight** comes on, on a horse. His **Servant** walks beside him.]

Knight: War isn't what it used to be.
Servant: No, sir.
Knight: Hardly pays the fare home.
Servant: Right sir.
Knight: We been plundering over there so long, there's nothing left
Servant: Right sir.
Knight: What with that and the plague.
Servant: Yes, sir.
Knight: The King's getting senile, the French've discovered gunpowder and we lose every time.
Servant: Right, sir.
Knight: Crécy was the high point. Calais. The good old days. If you want to win battles now, you've got to sit on your arse in Parliament.
Servant: Yes, sir.
Knight: All I want to do is retire to my manor and breed sheep.
Servant: Yes, sir.

[**A Bishop** comes on, carried pick-a-back by **A Serf,** who is learning The Ten Commandments in verse.]

Serf 1: One God in worship entertain.
Bishop: Yes.

8

Serf 1: Never take his name in vain.

Bishop: Good.

Serf 1: Keep and guard your holy day.

Bishop: Yes.

Serf 1: To father and mother honour pay.

Bishop: Right.

Serf 1: Murder of men put out of mind
Never sin with womankind
False oath swear not
False witness bear not
For wife of neighbour see you never lust
For goods of neighbour have no greed unjust.

Bishop: [rhetorically to **Knight** and **Servant**]

Good! are these commandments ten
Keep them strictly all you men
He who shall not keep them well
Shall go down to deepest hell
He who keeps them right
Shall go to heaven bright.

[He beams at **The Knight** and **The Servant**]

Knight: Bollocks.

Bishop: I beg your pardon.

Knight: You sit on your arses getting fat, and we protect you.

Bishop: Wrong: **we** protect **you**. From God's wrath for swearing. Have an indulgence. [He fumbles in his cassock.]

Knight: God gave his sheep to be pastured, not shaven and shorn.

Bishop: What does that mean?

Knight: There was a time when the Church looked after its people, gave alms to the poor. Now all you do is pay less wages than anyone else and work your way into all the top jobs.

Bishop: Have a relic.

Knight: You cream off discontent by educating all those clever enough to see through you, then to prove you're on a par with the barons, you dress like them and screw the same whores.

[Pause]

Bishop: You haven't been reading Wycliff by any chance?

Knight: He's got your measure.

Bishop: Sucking up to the King, that's all. Wants more money for his university.

Knight: To Caesar what is Caesar's, to God what is God's. The

Church has no right to temporal power or possessions. It started off poor, and that kept it honest.

Bishop: That may be what they teach at Oxford, but Wycliff wouldn't help a poor man any more than you would. The Church looks after its people. From right of sanctuary down to a steady wage and universal education.

Knight: One in a hundred isn't universal. And the wages are steady even when everybody else's go up. Your days are numbered, Bishop. Now labourers are free to go where wages are highest, you may find a few following strength [he shoulders his sword] not tradition.

Bishop: The privilege of working for the Church has always counted for more than high wages. If we were all-powerful, we'd be all-bountiful — like God. But sheep are better shorn than slaughtered. On foreign soil, at that.

Knight: A man can earn good money in the New Army.

Bishop: I suppose that's why most of them desert.

Knight: Agh ! [He doubles up in pain.]

Bishop: Trouble?

Knight: War-wound.

Bishop: God's judgement for insulting the Church. [He places his hand on the helpless **Knight's** head, makes a cross with the other hand and mutters a cure in Latin.] In nomine patris et filius et spiritus sanctus, hic curatus et sanatus. — Better?

[**The Knight** looks up, relieved.
The Bishop holds out his hand.]

Bishop: One mark, please.

[The scene breaks. **Someone** announces:]

1351: The Statute of Labourers

Against the malice of servants who were idle and unwilling to serve after the pestilence without taking outrageous wages, it was recently ordained by our Lord the King that such servants as carters, ploughmen, shepherds, swineherds, domestic and other servants shall be obliged to serve for the salaries and wages which were customary during the year of 1346. No-one is to receive more than a penny a day for weeding or hay-making, more than twopence halfpenny a day for threshing a quarter of wheat or rye, nor more than a penny halfpenny for a quarter of barley, beans or oats. Reapers of corn are to be limited to twopence, mowers to fivepence. Less is to be given where less used to be given and neither food nor favour is to be demanded, given or

taken. All workers are to bring their own tools to the
market towns, and men are to be hired in a public, and not
a secret place.

Carpenters, masons, tilers, thatchers, plasterers and workers
on mud walls shall not take more than threepence for their
day's work, and their boys a penny halfpenny. Cordwainers
and shoemakers shall not sell boots, shoes or anything
connected with their mystery other than they did in 1346.
Goldsmiths, saddlers, horse-smiths, tanners, tailors and all
other artisans shall conduct their crafts as they did in 1346.
Those same servants are not to depart from the vills in which
they live during the winter to serve elsewhere in the summer.
Stewards, bailiffs and constables of the vills shall inquire
diligently into all those who infringe this ordinance. They
are to give the names of offenders to the justices whenever
they arrive in a district to hold their sessions. Those who
refuse to take the oath, or fail to fulfil what they have
undertaken, shall be put in the stocks for three days or more,
or sent to the nearest gaol, there to remain until they are
willing to submit to justice. They shall pay fine and ransom
to the King if convicted. Offenders shall be imprisoned for
forty days, second offenders for a quarter of a year, so that
each time they are convicted, they shall receive double
penalty. No sheriffs, stewards or bailiffs shall receive anything
from the said servants, and justices shall enquire whether
they have concealed anything because of gifts, procurement
or affinity, and shall fine them if found guilty. These fines
shall be delivered to the collectors of taxes where these
subsidies are being levied. Justices shall hold sessions four
times a year, or more as necessary. Those who maintain or
encourage the said servants against this ordinance shall be
severely punished according to the discretion of the justices.
If any servant flee from one county to another because of
this ordinance, the sheriffs of the county where they are
found shall have them apprehended and brought to the chief
gaol of the said county. And this ordinance is to be held
within the city of London as in other boroughs through the
land, within franchise and without.

[**Three Serfs** run on. **The Announcer** goes off. **The Serfs** are
on the run from their manor.]

Serf 1: Come on !
Serf 2: I can't any more.
Serf 3: Leave him.
Serf 1: We can't.

11

Serf 3: They'll catch us else.

Serf 1: Stick together's best. Three fight better than one.

Serf 3: They got dogs. They'll be here in no time.

Serf 1: I need a rest anyway.

Serf 3: I don't.

Serf 1: Sitting duck on your own.

Serf 3: I'm not sitting. [He looks off.] Getting closer.

Serf 1: We could hide.

Serf 3: From dogs? You and me'll be all right.

Serf 1: Can't do that.

Serf 2: Go on.

Serf 1: It was your idea. Here. [He gives him something to drink.]

Serf 3: All right then, see you in London.

Serf 1: Yeh.

[**Serf 3** goes off]

Serf 2: You're mad.

Serf 1: He gets on my nerves. I ran away to be free. Chained to him's as bad as chained to the manor. What's the point of running away from Church land to earn a free wage if you can't spend it with mates of your own choosing? Sooner give myself up.

Serf 2: How close are they?

[**Serf 1** gets up and looks.]

Serf 1: Won't be long.

Serf 2: You hide then. I'll say you both left me.

Serf 1: Dogs, though. Like he said. Look, you have this.

[He gives him food, drink and a cloak.]

Serf 1: Cover yourself up. Right?

[**Serf 2** hides himself.]

Serf 1: I'll get up a tree. Might help.

[A terrible scream from the direction **Serf 3** went off.]

Serf 2: What's that?

Serf 1: The other way ! That's not them !

Serf 2: Quick !

[**Serf 1** hides. **Serf 3** staggers on. He has been branded with an 'F' on his forehead. He is followed by **A Monk** and **A Bailiff,** who carries a branding iron.]

Monk: I don't know why they run away. We give them ploughs, oxen, barns, the use of a mill and a bakery, and they do this to us. It never used to happen.

Bailiff: Lord Burley pays wages, though. Happening everywhere since the plague. Labour's so short.

Monk: Perhaps we ought to pay wages.

Bailiff: You'd still ask your manor dues, though. And rents. If they live a year in a town, they become free men by law. For nothing. You can't beat that. — All right, in here !

[He has unloaded a stocks from the cart, and **Serf 3** sits in them. He is weeping.]

Monk: Tears of repentance.

Serf 3: I could've murdered a man, you wouldn't do this to me!

Monk: Ingratitude, my son. You cannot bite the hand that feeds you.

Serf 3: If we bit the hand, it's because what's in it isn't enough.

Bailiff: They'd have your whole arm if they could.

Monk: No-one starves. If we paid wages, we'd have to stop providing meals. You wouldn't eat meat. You'd spend it all on ale.

[**Serf 3** sags in the stocks, silent.]

Monk: You need our guidance, our discipline. We relaxed fines because people were leaving. Now the work's shoddy. If I don't make an example of you, others will leave and no-one will work the land with which Mother Church has fed you for centuries.

[A bell tolls.]

Monk: Vespers. I must get back. Thank-you for your help.

Bailiff: I'll leave him here two days. Then I'll bring him back to you.

Monk: Very kind. Goodbye.

[**The Monk** hurries off. **The Bailiff** turns towards where **Serf 2** is hiding.]

Bailiff: Right, come out !

[No movement. **The Bailiff** kicks the bundle. **Serf 2** emerges.]

Serf 2: If you knew I was there, whyn't you turn me in?

Bailiff: I got plans for you. Whatever the bible says, a man **can** serve two masters.

Serf 2: What you mean?

Bailiff: Lord Burley's looking for reapers. Penny halfpenny a day.

Serf 2: It's twopence by The Statute.

Bailiff: Always give you back to the monks.

Serf 2: People are getting up to fivepence.

13

Bailiff: Not any more. There's a new law. The lords get a reduction
on their taxes for all fines they take from labourers
exceeding the Statute rate.

Serf 2: We can't fine them for their prices, though, can we. You pa
the same prices. What do you get out of it?

Bailiff: Bits and pieces here and there. Commission on you.

Serf 2: He coming? [**Serf 3** in the stocks.]

Bailiff: He's known now. More than my job's worth to let him go.

Serf 2: Look at him.

Bailiff: I know. The Church are the last pagans.

Serf 2: Why d'you work for them then, traitor.

Bailiff: It's this or back to penny halfpenny a day for reaping. And
don't call me names. That monk would've had his head off

Serf 2: What's the difference? He's done for anyway.

Bailiff: Keeps his nose clean, he'll be all right. Where's the other one

Serf 2: What?

Bailiff: Three of you. Don't kid me.

Serf 2: They both left me. Went with him.

[**The Bailiff** turns to **Serf 3** in the stocks.]

Serf 3: We split up.

[**The Bailiff** doesn't believe them.]

Bailiff: All right, I've had enough for one day anyway.

Serf 2: Who was them with dogs then?

Bailiff: Dogs? Don't tell me there's poachers too.

Serf 2: Richer'n poachers.

Bailiff: My lord hunting then.

Serf 2: I thought he was harvesting.

Bailiff: Not him, mate. You. On your feet.

Serf 2: I've hurt my ankle.

Bailiff: Have to be better tomorrow. We start at five.

Serf 2: I haven't done so bad then, after all.

Bailiff: What about these? [The cloak and bag with food, etc.]

Serf 2: Not mine.

[**The Bailiff** looks around. He sees nothing.]

Bailiff: Come on then !

[They go off. Pause. **Serf 1** comes out of hiding.]

Serf 1: Need anything?

Serf 3: Fuck off.

Serf 1: I'll leave these. [He leaves the bag with food, etc.]

Serf 3: Just fuck off.

14

[**Serf 1** picks up the bag and cloak. He turns to the audience and sings 'The Song of The London Lickpenny'. Behind him the scene breaks.]

Serf 1: To London once my steps I bent
where truth in no wise should be faint,
to Westminsterward I forthwith went
to a man of law to make complaint.
I said 'For Mary's love, that holy saint,
pity the poor that would proceed.'
But, for lack of money, I could not speed.
And as I thrust the presse among
by forward chance my hood was gone,
yet for all that I stayed not long
till at the King's Bench I was come;
before the judge I kneeled anon
and prayed him for God's sake to take heed.
But, for lack of money, I could not speed.

Unto the Rolls I gat me from thence
before the clerks of the Chancelry,
where many I found earning of pence
but none at all once regarded me.
I gave them my plaint upon my knee;
they liked it well when they had it read
but, lacking money, I could not be sped.

Within this hall neither rich nor poor
would do for me ought, although I should die,
which seeing I gat me out of the door,
where Flemings began for to cry :
'Master, what will you copen or buy?
Fine felt hats or spectacles to read?
Lay down your silver and here you may speed.'

Then into London I did me hie
of all the land it beareth the prize.
'Hot peascods' one began to cry,
'Strawberry ripe' and 'Cherries in the rice!'
One bad me come near and buy some spice.
I never was used to such things indeed
and, wanting money, I might not speed.

Then into Cornhill anon I yode
where was much stolen gear among
I saw where hung my own hood
that I had lost among the throng

to buy my own hood I thought it wrong
I knew it well as I did my creed
but, for lack of money, I could not speed.

[In London **The Master** brings in **Serf 1** and introduces him
to his new work situation. **Two Journeymen** sit combing
and preparing wool.]

Master: Right then, you'll work here with these two. They'll tell you
what to do. They're good lads, work hard. See you do too.

[He goes. Long silence. **The Journeymen** and **Serf 1** look at
each other. **Serf 1** nods and grunts indistinctly, then clears
his throat.]

Serf 1: Morning.
Journeyman 1: Come to join us, have you?
Serf 1: 'Sright.
Journeyman 2: What's your name?
Serf 1: Christopher. Southfen.
Journeyman 1: Where you from, Christopher?
Serf 1: Oh. Around.
Journeyman 2: Country?

[Pause.]

Serf 1: Yes.
Journeyman 1: Friends of mine been trying to work here two years.
Londoners, what's more.
Journeyman 2: The guild don't like 'foreigners'.
Serf 1: I know. The master said he had relatives, though, where I
come from.
Journeyman 1: Experienced hands these were. Put out of work by Flemmies.
Journeyman 2: You done the work before?
Serf 1: No.
Journeyman 1: Run away, did you?

[Pause.]

Eh?
Serf 1: Mind your own.
Journeyman 2: We won't run you in. We just want to know.
Serf 1: I came to London to be free. No work, no lodgings. Free
to starve. I spent three weeks begging and thieving just to
keep myself smart. I knew I'd not get work if I looked dirty.
Journeyman 1: Enterprise.
Serf 1: I was lucky.
Journeyman 1: Too right you were. It's only because a fella left last week
he's taken anyone on now. This last bloke was too

16

	ambitious. Wanted to be a master himself. Even tried it on with the Old Man's daughter.
Serf 1:	I just want to work, that's all.
Journeyman 2:	Everyone's on the make now, see. It's a big scramble. Even the Old Man himself. He never comes in the shop himself these days. Off in the city, chatting up the big cloth merchants. Looking for a market abroad. It's not easy. The victualling guilds've got the run of London. Fishmongers and grocers. Give the King a rake-off and he's in the palm of your hand. Foreign trade's nothing to a victualler. And they don't employ people like the wool men, so they're more popular. Which gets up John of Gaunt's nose and don't make life easy for our Old Man.
Journeyman 1:	So he likes people under him who know their place. And so do we. Only for different reasons.
Journeyman 2:	Big fish get bigger, and we're stuck where we are. Journeymen can't set up as their own masters these days, let alone export the stuff. That's all changed. So we got to make sure we do all right as we are.
Serf 1:	I'm all for that.
Journeyman 1:	Yeh?

[**The Master** comes back on.]

| **Master:** | I said teach him the ropes, not stand around chatting. |
| **Journeyman 2:** | Your job'll be cleaning. Picking out the grass and grit in the wool. Use these. |

[He holds up a pair of tweezers.]

| **Journeyman 2:** | Then it's got to be washed, combed and carded. I'll show you where everything's kept. You'll take care of deliveries too. |

[**The Master** goes.]

Journeyman 2:	Understand though, we're craftsmen. If you can't be your own master any more, then skill must be recognised. You won't get a fair wage by fighting your friends for it.
Serf 1:	When I ran away I was with two blokes, but we split up. I said that we should stick together.
Journeyman 1:	That's right. There's a meeting end of the week. We call ourselves The Sons of Jesus, so we're not suspected. We say prayers, light candles, then talk about how we're to protect our interests. You coming?
Serf 1:	Yes.
Journeyman 2:	I'll show you the loom.

17

[The scene breaks. Several **Actors** dressed as **London Merchants** come on, pushing the cart and carrying torches. It is evening. They sing 'For thou art comen of good blood'.

For thou art comen of good blood
For thou art a rich man of good
For thou art well loved of more
And for thou art a young man also

For thou art comen of rich blood
And for thou art a rich man also
For thou art well loved of more
And for thou art a rich man also

If thou art rich then thou art free
If thou be poor then woe is thee
For but thou spend it well ere thou go
Thy song for ever is well I woe!

[As they sing they position the cart under the balcony, where **Prince Richard** enters with his **Mother** and holds wool while she winds. The song finishes. **Someone** announces:]

**Spring 1377: As Edward the Third declines,
the Victualling Guilds of London
seek to win the favour of the young Prince Richard,
heir to the throne.**

[**Philpot,** one of the Merchants, climbs up on to the cart and peers into the balcony.]

Bramber: Is he there?
Philpot: He's with his mother. Winding wool.
Walworth: What?!
Bramber: Perhaps we shouldn't, then.
Walworth: Go on!
Philpot: God save Prince Richard from ill-health, and may he become a just and honourable sovereign over our realm!

[He bows. **Richard** comes to see who it is.]

Philpot: Your Highness, in the interests of the future peace of London, and at the suggestion of John of Gaunt, Duke of Lancaster, that the victualling guilds of London make their peace with him and the future King of England, we should like to invite His Royal Highness to a small game of chance. We assure him that should he win, the rewards will not be meagre.

[**The Merchants** are carrying their gifts openly.]

Richard: Really?

Philpot: The game is called dice, your Highness. Would you allow me to demonstrate, sir, by rolling first?

Richard: Please.

Philpot: John Philpot, sir, of the Fishmongers' Guild versus Richard of Bordeaux!

[He rolls.]

Philpot: A three! Three for the Fishmongers of London! Now you, your Highness. Richard's dice, please!

[A Boy Assistant hands over the dice. Richard still has the wool on his hands.]

Philpot: You'll have to put your wool down, sir.

Richard: Yes, of course. [He does so, takes the dice and rolls.]

Philpot: Twelve! Twelve for Richard of Bordeaux!

[Hefty applause.]

Philpot: You win, your Highness. The prize, this cup of pure gold. From the Fishmongers of London.

Richard: Thank-you. This is more fun than holding wool.

Philpot: We're glad you think so, sir. Another round?

Richard: Yes please!

Philpot: Nicholas Bramber, sir, of the Grocers' Guild. Versus Richard of Bordeaux!

[Bramber steps up, bows and rolls.]

Philpot: A five! Five for the Grocers of London! Now you, your Highness.

[Richard picks up Bramber's dice.]

Philpot: Not those, your Highness. Those are the victuallers' dice. These are yours.

Richard: Oh?

[Richard looks at Philpot. Philpot beams.
Richard rolls the dice.]

Philpot: Twelve again! Twelve for Richard of Bordeaux!

[Hefty applause.]

Bramber: Your Highness, the Grocers' Guild of London has pleasure in presenting you with this magnificent jewelled ring.

Richard: How lovely! Again please.

19

Philpot: Ahh! With pleasure, your Highness. William Walworth, sir, of the Butchers' Guild — versus Richard of Bordeaux!

Richard: Can I throw first this time?

Philpot: By all means, your Highness.

[**Richard** rolls.]

Richard: Oh. Seven.

Philpot: Are you sure? Oh. Seven for Prince Richard!

[Tentative, then faked applause. Sweating, **Walworth** throws

Assistant: Eight!

Richard: What?

[**Walworth** turns a die over.]

Philpot: Four! Four for the Butchers!

Richard: [Arms outstretched.] My prize please.

Walworth: On behalf of the Butchers' Guild of London, your Highness, may I present you with this silver plate, set with rubies and emeralds.

Richard: Ohhh!

Philpot: Your future Majesty, the victualling guilds of London declare themselves well and truly beaten. They hope they have proved themselves loyal and trustworthy servants of the Royal Family and their friends, and that, all past differences settled, when they next play with the King, it will be for even higher stakes.

Richard: That would be very nice. I shan't forget this game.

Philpot: Your Highness, we beg leave to retire now.

Richard: Thank-you.

[He gives a curt wave and picks up his prizes. **The Queen Mother** offers him the wool.]

Richard: No, Mummy, look.

[He shows her the prizes. **The Victuallers** retire, taking the cart with them and singing the second verse of 'For thou ar comen of good blood'. **Someone** announces:]

June 1377: Alice Perrers and John of Gaunt
visit the dying Edward the Third

[On the balcony **Edward III** is horizontal and dying. **Alice Perrers** and **John of Gaunt** come in on tip-toe.]

Alice: [Whispering.] Has he gone?

Edward: Not quite, Alice.

[**Edward** pulls **Alice** down on himself and kisses her. She
gives a little scream, then pulls herself away.]

Edward: No-one loves a dead king.
John: We're your only friends, father. Everyone else is fawning
round young Richard.
Edward: Good. As long as they're not fawning round you, John.
John: That's not fair, father. I've worked hard for that boy and his
throne.
Edward: You've had to. Or all London would've risen and had your
head off. If you were really interested in that boy, you'd
have given him some of your own land. You own a third of
this country as it is.
Alice: Edward, can you hear me? I've brought some papers for
you to sign. A pardon for Wykeham. Why don't you give
him back his land? Mmm? It's ten years since he was
Chancellor anyway.
Edward: The man was corrupt! [To **John.**] She screwing him?
Alice: I'll be here tonight, darling, don't worry.
Edward: I might not last that long.
Alice: I've got the papers here. All you have to do is seal them.
Edward: Why should I?
Alice: Too tired, darling? Let me.

[She grabs the seal-ring on **Edward's** finger.]

Edward: Get off!
Alice: Come on then, I'll help you.

[She melts wax. **Edward** presses the seal.]

Edward: There. And don't say I wasn't generous to you. 3,000 a
year, that's more pocket-money than my entire parliament
enjoys. Not to mention those little favours to your friends.
Alice: [Kissing **Edward.**] You've been wonderful, darling. [She tries
to withdraw a ring as she embraces him.]
Edward: Enough!
John: You may have been wonderful to her, darling, but I've had
to fight for everything I got.
Edward: Don't complain, John. You got fat while my good son
Edward was plundering the French for me. He died an
honourable soldier's death.
John: Yes, dysentery and dropsy.
Edward: And that's why his son's getting the throne, not you. If I'd
made you King, there'd have been no stopping you.
John: Would that have been bad?
Edward: I thought you had your eye on Castile.

John: It fell through.

Edward: Just as well. You'd have had all Europe. One country's enough for any man. [He dies.]

Alice: Too much.

John: That's it.

Alice: What?

John: He's gone.

Alice: No!

John: Anything you want before I call the others?

Alice: One moment. [She pulls the rings from **Edward's** fingers.]

John: Not that one. [The seal. He pockets it.]

Alice: What will you do now, John?

John: See Richard settled in, then get out of it. London hates me. The only friends I've got are up North. A border expedition might be just the thing. Richard'll let me go. I'll have my own trained army, and if trouble blows up down here, I'll be well out of the shooting. Come on, let's get this over with

[They go. **Someone** walks on and announces:]

Before John of Gaunt left London, he set in motion through Parliament, a new form of levying money for the Crown. A subsidy of four pence per head from all persons, rich and poor alike, throughout the land. **The First Poll Tax.**

[A village ale-house. Sunday evening. **Will,** the local priest, is talking to **Matt,** the innkeeper.]

Will: I tell you, Matt, thighs on her like tree-trunks. It's all that spinning on the foot-treadle. Develops the muscles.

Matt: That's no way for a priest to talk about a woman, Will.

Will: Ah, come on!

Matt: And her married too.

Will: Her husband's an idiot. Odo had one of his strips away last year and he didn't say a thing. Everyone with a strip next to his ploughs a furrow of it into their own.

Matt: You mean: you do.

Will: Move the marker stone across, it hardly shows. He can't understand why his yield gets less every year. That's why she's taken to spinning. Bolster their income.

Matt: Last year it was her sister you were laying.

Will: Her husband was an idiot too. Pickin' 'em must run in the family. It was when that one got pregnant I met this sister.

Matt: You christened that child.

That's what I'm paid for! Christen 'em when they're born, settle their rows while they're alive and bury 'em when they're dead. What more do you want?

Matt: You might hold a service now and again.

Will: Three I've missed! Three this year. That's better than many. — Here. [He pushes his mug across. **Matt** fills it.] Anyway, what you expect on the stipend the bishop pays me? If I didn't farm a few strips and go to market, I'd be the poorest man in the vill. That's not what my old man had me educated for.

Matt: The first Christians were paupers.

Will: I'm sorry I taught you that. Don't forget I got an assistant to pay — and my housekeeper, my hearthmate.

Matt: 'Hearth-mate', that's good. Where d'you lay all these women if she's round the house all day?

Will: Where d'you think?

Matt: You use that building for everything but praying in. Can't get in the door of a weekday for chicken and geese.

Will: They got to have a roof over 'em.

Matt: Build 'em a coop then.

Will: I'm too busy.

Matt: Yeh, threshing corn in the vestry, I know.

Will: When?

Matt: Last autumn.

Will: It was raining!

Matt: No wonder half the windows are broken.

Will: You go on like this, I'll take my custom elsewhere.

Matt: I wish you would. If there was another ale-house in the vill, I might make a bit of profit.

Will: You and me, Matt, have got only one thing in common. We both got our markets tied up.

[**Thomas** and **Siward,** peasants, **Odo,** a ploughman, and an **Out-of-town Preacher** come on. **The Preacher** might be John Ball.]

Thomas: Evening Will, Matt.

Matt: Evening Thomas. — Looks like you got competition after all, Will.

Will: It's all right for the travellers. They ain't got a building to look after and the same flock to tend all the time.

Preacher: My flock is the whole country, brother.

Will: Better to tend a few well than to scant many, brother.

Preacher: The man who travels sees more than the stay-at-home.

Will: All he sees is the top-soil, though.

Preacher: Depends on the man.

Will: You weren't in church this evening, gentlemen.

Odo: Were you?

Will: Now, that's enough!

Siward: Sunday evenings is ladies' service anyway.

Odo: We were in this morning.

Thomas: Been contemplating with the preacher, Will. On the hills.

Will: Oh yeh?

Matt: Walking the dogs, they call it.

Thomas: We took the dogs.

Will: Catch anything?

Thomas: Show him. He don't mind.

[**The Preacher** has been holding a rabbit out of sight. He] holds it up. **Will** inspects it.]

Will: Got some flesh on it.

Thomas: Sunday dinner. You're invited.
Wouldn't mind.

Thomas: Buy us a drink then.

Will: Hah! All right.

[**Matt** brings drinks. **Will** pays.]

Will: So. Good hunting.

Thomas· We'll have better soon.

Will: You're not starting that again.

Thomas: They can't grab taxes like that and expect us not to grab back, Will. Each new tax is an added burden. Buying personal land is the same thing written small. It helps you live better, but it's bought out of common land. That means less grazing land for those who can't afford to buy their own It's grabbing luxury at the poor's expense.

Will: You grabbed some yourself, Thomas.

Thomas: That was before everyone started. I didn't see what it meant then. There's hardly any common land left now. And for some, that's all they've got.

Will: You ain't given your land up though, that I've noticed.

Thomas: Who'd I give it up to? My lord? He'd buy it back cheaper than he sold it. As it is, I can give some of my crop to those who need it.

Will: Because they're too idle to work for themselves?

Preacher: Brother, I thought you were a church man.

Will: So I am. But I'm a peasant too. I believe in a good day's labour.

Preacher: I've never met a man who said he didn't. Not even a lord. We do the work, though. Do they?

Will: I'm not my lord's keeper.

Preacher: You're these people's keeper, though. And when we were all in loin cloths, there was no-one in velvet then, and no-one in poor rags. There was no-one who ate meat and white

24

bread and drank red wine every day, while others had potage, rye bread and thin ale. While we're out working in wind and rain, they sit in their manors with fires blazing. Of wood grown on God's soil, which is now suddenly their soil. Are they God? We're their slaves, that's certain. And there's no-one to protect us. Things can't go well in England till all things are in common.

Will: That's John Ball's teaching.

Preacher: And I go along with him.

Will: He's a madman.

Thomas: If any try buying common land at the next manor court, Will, we'll band together against it. If needs be, we'll put our money together and hire a lawyer. It's no good, each of us out for himself. I thought I was doing nicely till this new tax. Now all I've gained over the last two years is set back.

Odo: It's the same for labourers. I'm earning eight shillings a year now . . .

Will: Are you? You can buy us a drink then.

Odo: All right. — Matt! — But listen: eight shillings now, but by the Statute that's the limit. And the cost of things still goes up. People can't do like your father any more, Will. Buy their freedom and have their son educated by the Church. We're even forbidden to hold meetings. They're making money out of us to pay John of Gaunt's soldiers to plunder Europe, which does us no good at all.

Siward: He should know. He deserted.

Preacher: How long were you in?

Odo: Five weeks.

Will: Five weeks!

Odo: Why should I go abroad? I heard they stopped paying you once you were over there, so when we got to Dover, about twenty of us slipped off.

Will: Don't they keep an eye on you?

Odo: It's chaos getting on the ships. I got six weeks' money — nine shillings. They give you the first week abroad in advance — to encourage you.

Will: So you stole the King's money.

Odo: The King's money? Yours and mine. It was that or have the army steal my time.

Thomas: And they can pick him up any time. And reclaim free labourers as serfs. Unless we stand up as a vill and swear for them in the manor court. It's only when we act together we're strong.

Will: But a weak man when you're harvesting can put you back hours.

Thomas: He's got to eat too.

Will: As things are now each man gets his just reward. When the corn's in and our lord lets you take for your own what hay you can lift on your scythe, that's fair reward for the strength of a man's arm.

Preacher: Can you lift that?

[He points to a bale of straw.]

Will: You betting?

Preacher: Pint of ale says you can't.

Will: You're on.

[**Will** makes a good stab, but fails.]

Will: Matt, a pint for the preacher.

Preacher: Wait. There's four of you. Take all four bundles. Put those two poles underneath. One of you on each corner.

[They do this.]

Preacher: Now lift.

[They do it.]

Preacher: You tell me now who's the strong man.

[A bell rings out. The scene breaks. **Actors** come on, grab cloaks and become **Members of Parliament.** They sing 'Christ may send now such a year'.]

Another year it may betide
This company to be full wide
And never an order to abide
Christ may send now such a year.

Another year it may befall
The least that is within this hall
To be more master than us all
Christ may send now such a year.

These lords that been wonder great
They threaten power men for to beat
It lendeth little in their threat
Christ may send now such a year.

[When the song finishes, the bell is still sounding and **The Members of Parliament** hurry to take up their places. At the Half Moon this was amongst the audience.
Someone announces:]

26

8th November, 1380:
Parliament sits at Northampton

[**Sir John Gildesburgh,** Leader of the Commons, sits centrally amongst the audience. He introduces **Sudbury,** who is on stage.]

Gildesburgh: Pray silence, gentlemen, for Lord Sudbury, Archbishop of Canterbury and Chancellor of England.

Sudbury: Gentlemen, the Earl of Buckingham's military expedition to France has cost the King all you gave him at our last parliament and much of his own money. Moreover, because of John of Gaunt's expedition to Scotland and the money due to the Earl of March for Ireland, the King's jewels have been placed in pledge and are on the point of being lost. Nothing has been received from the subsidy of wools because of present rioting in Flanders, and the wages of our soldiers in Calais, Brest and Cherbourg being nine months in arrears, there is great danger they might leave. Finally there are the outrageous expenses necessary to safeguard our sea-coasts better this year than last. The King would welcome your advice as to how these expenses could best be met.

Gildesburgh: Archbishop Sudbury, much though we appreciate the efforts of the Earl and the Duke and hope the war will soon come to a profitable end for England, the Commons would appreciate a clearer statement of the total sum demanded of them, bearing in mind the present depleted state of the nation's pocket.

Sudbury: Sir John, a rough schedule of the sum necessary for the Commons' attention has been drawn up by the Lords. It amounts to 160,000 pounds.

[Shocked pause, then mingled hostile reactions from **The Commons:**]

Gildesburgh: 160,000 pounds?
Knight: Impossible!
Merchant: That's ridiculous!
Bishop: Monstrous!
Knight: We haven't got it, even if we approved it.
Bishop: Damned cheek.
Gildesburgh: Lord Simon, as Chancellor you must be aware that 160,000 pounds is completely insupportable by the Commons. I would suggest the sum be reduced to only what is absolutely necessary, unless you can indicate to us by what means such a sum might be levied.

27

Sudbury: Sir John, the Lords have already considered this issue at length and have arrived at three alternatives for the Commons to consider. First, that a sum of groats should be levied from every person in the kingdom.

Gildesburgh: Another Poll Tax.

Sudbury: Yes.

Knight: You know what happened with the last two, Lord Simon. Widespread evasion. The people won't co-operate. Out of an estimated 37,000 pounds on the First Poll Tax, only 22,000 were collected. The second graduated tax was even less efficient.

Gildesburgh: What other alternatives do the Lords suggest, sir?

Sudbury: The traditional levying of tithes and fifteenths.

Knight: Quite impossible. Taxes on land are an intolerable burden on the poor, not to mention those of us with considerable property of our own.

Sudbury: Or a tax on the pound of every kind of merchandise bought and sold within the kingdom, as and when the commodities are sold.

[Ugly pause, then hostile reactions.]

Merchant: Well!

Knight: There's gratitude for you!

Merchant: As if our money wasn't bailing the country out already!

[He stands.]

Lord Simon, a tax on trade would punish the merchant class — to which most of us here belong — unnecessarily and unfairly. Particularly since what little wealth the country possesses depends almost entirely on our energy and goodwill. It seems to me that by any other means than a Poll Tax, the new class of labourers and artisans get off far too lightly. We're being forced to pay them wages, and yet they contribute nothing to the nation's defence.

[Applause and assent from **The Commons**.]

Gildesburgh: Whichever method we use, 160,000 pounds, I think, is out of the question. The Commons might consent to a sum of, say, 100,000, if the clergy, who after all own a third of all the land in the realm, could say how much it is prepared to give.

Bishop: Sir John Gildesburgh, the clergy never makes its grant to the King within Parliament, nor should laymen constrain the clergy to do so. The liberty of The Holy Church should be respected and the Commons do their duty to their King.

[Pause.]

Bishop: However, considering the present great necessity, I feel bound to say that the clergy will certainly do as it ought — as it always has in the past — and might possibly be persuaded to raise the sum of 34,000 pounds.

Legge: In that case, gentlemen, I think I have the answer — John Legge, sergeant-at-arms to John of Gaunt, Duke of Lancaster. The collection of a third poll tax can be made more efficient by the establishment of commissions of enquiry into the returns of each individual vill. If carried out with determination this will remedy the objection of evasion quite rightly mentioned by the member earlier. Now, if the Church says it will raise 34,000 pounds, that leaves 66,000 pounds to be levied by the Commons. The first poll tax of a groat from each person in the realm raised 22,000 pounds. Therefore a tax of three groats per person will raise three times 22,000 pounds, 66,000 pounds, which is exactly the sum we require.

[Pause.]

Merchant: [Admiring.] Very good.

Knight: Couldn't have put it better myself.

Bishop: Who is that young man?

Knight: One of Gaunt's roughnecks, I believe.

Gildesburgh: Gentlemen, I think we agree that solves our problem. There remains nothing but to draw up the details. Parliament is adjourned and refreshment will be served in the White Swan Inn adjacent.

[**Everyone** off.]

[We took our interval here — The White Swan is the pub next to The Half Moon. After the interval the three bailiffs of the towns of **Fobbing, Corringham** and **Stanford** come on, pushing the cart. They stand to one side. A **Sergeant-at-Arms** comes on with a stool which he places on the cart. **Someone** announces:]

30th May, 1381: Brentwood, Essex

[**The Sergeant-at-Arms** stands on the cart and calls out:]

Sergeant: Oyez, oyez. Because following the granting of a subsidy to the King of a shilling per head from all lay persons in the realm over the age of fifteen, the collectors of the said subsidy have spared many persons, partly through negligence, partly through favour, the King has appointed John Bampton, our lord's steward and commissioner for the area, to call together this day the bailiffs of the townships of Fobbing, Corringham and Stanford, that they present for inspection all indentures concerning the assessment and collection of the said subsidy. And be it understood that the said John Bampton is authorised to seize and arrest all whom he finds acting in opposition or rebellion to the above commands, and that such persons are to be held in prison until provision is made for their punishment.

[He steps down from the cart. **John Bampton** comes on and sits on the stool on the cart.]

Bampton: Is the bailiff of Corringham present?

Corring: Here.

Bampton: Can you provide me with a statement of the number of people over the age of fifteen in your village?

Corring: I got it on here. [He holds out a stick, heavily notched.]

Bampton: What's that?

Corring: That's the books.

Bampton: Explain yourself.

Corring: I count on that. When folk are born, I make a notch down the side. When they die, I put a cross through. When I run out of stick, I get a new one.

Bampton: Can't you write?

Corring: The vill's re-elected me bailiff thirteen times. People trust me, even my lord. It's quicker in the long run.

Bampton: Thomas Baker of Fobbing.

Baker: Here.

Bampton: Can you provide me with a written statement of the names and number of people over the age of fifteen in your village?

Baker: No I can't.

Bampton: Why not?

Baker: We paid that tax already.

Bampton: This is not a new tax. We're trying to find out the defaulter on the old one, that's all. You're responsible.

Baker: I did away with that list after we paid the last time. I didn't think we'd have to pay again.

Bampton: You are not paying again! I want those names.

Baker: You'd only get the same names as last time. The defaulters'll still go free and those who paid before'll have to pay again. It don't make our job any easier. A shilling's two weeks' work for some of our people. Pay that twice, with manor dues, tithes and fifteenths, and that's half a year's money. [To **Corringham** and **Stanford**.] All to keep John of Gaunt in pocket.

Bampton: Hold your tongue. You heard what was read out. I'm commissioned by the King to re-assess this tax. By whichever means seems most expedient. It's people like you who cause these discrepancies. I can have you thrown in jail.

Baker: That won't help me find more money. You put us in jail if we ask more money for our work, too. How we going to pay more dues if we can't earn more wages?

Bampton: Do I get a list of names or not?

Baker: No. We got a receipt from you last time we paid, and that's enough. For all we know you might've creamed some off yourself.

Bampton: [To **Sergeant**.] Arrest this man.

[**The Three Bailiffs** draw closer together and draw knives.]

Stanford: [To **Sergeant**.] You try it.

Bampton: What is this?

Baker: We're not paying twice.

Bampton: This is strictly illegal.

Stanford: The law suits you because you make it. It don't suit us.

Bampton: I shall have you flogged! All of you!

Baker: Come on then.

Bampton: Ruffians!

Corring: No need for names, now.

Bampton: You can't evade this tax for ever, you know!

Baker: Now'll do. If you go now, we shan't hurt you.

[**Bampton** and **The Sergeant** go.]

Corring: They went too!

Stanford: I told you.

Baker: We done it now.

Corring: Who'd have thought it.

Stanford: Just goes to show, though.

Baker: What happens now?

Stanford: They'll be back, that's what. With soldiers.

Baker: I better make myself scarce then.

Stanford: If you want help, Tom, my folk are willing.

Corring: And mine.

Baker: Fight 'em, you mean?

Stanford: I could have 'em here by Saturday. Show 'em we mean it.

Corring: That'll surprise 'em.

Baker: Why not?

Corring: In for a penny.

Stanford: You sure now?

Baker: No point in going back on ourselves.

Stanford: You keep in the woods, then. You got food all right?

Baker: Yeh.

31

Stanford: We'll see you here then, Saturday.

> [**Corringham** and **Stanford** go off. **Baker** sings the first verse of 'The Song of The Yorkshire Partisans'.]

Baker: In the Country hard was we
that in our district shrewes should be
with all support to make
Among the friars it is so
and other orders many more
whether they sleep or wake.

> [As the song finishes, the men of **Stanford** and **Corringham** return. They are now armed.]

Stanford: We'll stay out front. You keep back, and draw him on.

> [The men of **Stanford** and **Corringham** lie in ambush. **Justice Bealknap** bursts on with two heavily-armed guards.]

Bealknap: I'm Justice Bealknap. I've been sent on a commission of trailbaston. Where's Tom Baker?

Baker: Here.

> [**Bealknap** walks forward. The men of **Stanford** and **Corringham** ambush and surround **The Guards**. **Baker** holds a bible.]

Baker: Justice Bealknap, swear on this bible never again to act as justice on inquests of this kind against the poor commons.

Bealknap: I swear.

Baker: We want the names of those who were to serve as jurors for these sessions.

Bealknap: Here. [He gives **Baker** a list.]

Baker: You can go now.

> [**Bealknap** goes. **The Rebels** bundle **The Guards** off. **Baker** holds the list up.]

Baker: We'll have the head of every person on this list. Every lawyer, juror and royal servant from John Legge down who helped make this evil tax. We'll carry their heads in front of us as a warning and burn every last record of our slavery. It won't be us hiding in the woods any more.

> [**Two Rebels** come back on with the guards' heads on poles, accompanied by **Thomas Farringdon**. He is better dressed than the peasants. They fall silent.]

Farringdon: My name's Thomas Farringdon. I've come from London with a letter for you from John Ball in Maidstone Jail. [He reads] 'John Carter prays you all that you make good end of what you have begun, and do well and even better. For by the evening men hear the day, and if the end is well, then all is well. Look that Hobb the Robber be well chastened for leasing of your grace, for you have need to take God with you in all your deeds. Now is time to beware.' Hobb the Robber, Sir Robert Hales, Treasurer of England, has robbed me of my inheritance and seized my tenements. Twenty miles from here his country manor, Cressing Temple, is crammed full of food and wine. Those of you who wish to celebrate today's victory, and revenge me, could find no better place.

Baker: We've done a good day's work today. We deserve a reward. But some of us must take messages to our people in Kent, and in Suffolk and Norfolk. They'll want to know what's happened here.

Stanford: [holding up a flagon of wine] Courtesy of Justice Robert Bealknap!

[**A Peasant** takes it and drinks.]

Peasant 2: Come on then, don't hog it all!

Baker: Let's go.

[A regular, heavy drumbeat begins. **Someone** comes forward and sings the second verse of 'The Yorkshire Partisans':]

All men may come and go
among us to and fro
I say most surely
but teasing we will suffer none
neither of Hobb nor of John
whatever man he be.

[They all go off. **Someone** announces:]

3rd June: Gravesend

[**Sir Simon Burley** comes in.]

Burley: Bring him here!

[He is followed by **Two Sergeants-at-Arms,** who bring in **Robert Belling,** whose hands are tied. They are followed by **Three Citizens of Gravesend.**]

Citizen 1: Sir Simon, this is an insult to Gravesend and an encroachment on the privileges of the town. We're a free borough and make our own laws, subject to no-one but the King himself.

Burley: The King's a weakling. I know this man. He's my serf.

Citizen 2: Lord Burley, Robert Belling is a free citizen of Gravesend.

33

He's lived with us longer than a year, and by the law of the land he owes obeisance to no master.

Burley: He's a trouble-maker. There's been too much running away lately. It's becoming the fashion. Servants think they can do what they like. Run away for a year and think that makes them different. I own this man.

Citizen 1: We're willing to pay for his freedom, Sir Simon. We protect our people. Belling's worked well for this town. He'll pay us back.

Burley: Buy him, eh. Do you know what he's cost me in loss of work days? In goods removed? In loss of any wife he might've taken? Not to mention others who've followed his example.

Citizen 1: That's for you to decide.

Burley: Three hundred pounds.

[Pause.]

Belling: That's ridiculous. I couldn't have earned that in a lifetime on your land.

Burley: I've named my price. If the town of Gravesend wishes to protect this man, it should put its money where its pitiful civic pride is. Otherwise your pleading is hot air.

Citizen 1: We can't pay three hundred pounds. You should ask some more reasonable sum.

Burley: Lock him up.

[**Robert Belling** is put in stocks.]

Burley: I'm taking this man to Rochester Castle. As an escaped serf. When you've got three hundred pounds, you can have him back.

[**Burley, Belling** and the **Two Sergeants** go.]

Citizen 1: Well.

Citizen 2: I told you.

Citizen 3: If Simon Burley can do that, the King's charter of freedom to Gravesend is a mockery.

Citizen 2: Unless you can take two of those sergeants with you wherever you go, the law is nothing but paper.

Citizen 1: Might beats right.

Citizen 2: You see.

Citizen 3: You know what happened in Brentwood, don't you.

Citizen 1: What?

Citizen 3: When the commissioner came to collect the poll tax again because there'd been fiddling, they banded together and chased him off.

34

Citizen 2: Then what?

Citizen 3: The Royal Council sent a Justice of the Peace in. With troops.

Citizen 2: Of course.

Citizen 3: They surrounded the troops and chased the Justice off. People are rising all over Essex. They say the tax is unjust.

Citizen 1: But we've paid our tax. We're in the right. We've done nothing illegal.

Citizen 2: Perhaps it's time we did. Everyone else is, it seems.

Citizen 3: Remember John Ball: we were all born the same. How can a King give you what's yours by rights anyway?

Citizen 2: He can take it away again, that's clear.

Citizen 3: A king is king by law. If he breaks the law, he's no king. We should go to Rochester and take Robert Belling back.

Citizen 1: We could try.

Citizen 3: Let's find the others.

> [They go off. The drumbeat sounds again.
> **Someone** comes forward and sings the third verse of
> 'The Yorkshire Partisans':]

And yet will each one help another
and maintain him as his brother
both in wrong and right
And also will we stand and stir
to maintain our neighbour
with all our might.

> [As the song finishes, **Someone** announces:]

3rd June: Dartford

> [**John Tyler**, his **Wife** and **Daughter** come in, followed by
> **A Tax-Collector** and **A Sergeant-at-Arms**.]

Collector: Line up!

> [**The Family** stands in a line.]

Collector: Name?

Tyler: John Tyler.

Collector: This your entire family?

Tyler: All that's lived.

Collector: Who's she?

Tyler: Our daughter.

Collector: No tax paid on her.

Tyler: She's not fifteen.

Collector: Looks it to me.

Tyler: Fourteen.

Collector: Never! [He laughs.]

Tyler: We had her, we fed her, kept her out of trouble. We should know.

Collector: You know I'm empowered to use whatever means necessary to collect this tax from defaulters?

Tyler: So I've heard.

Collector: We're sorting out the parasites, scrounging off the rest of us.

Tyler: My lord has forty-five work days a year from me for nothing It's not me that's scrounging.

Collector: I don't believe that girl's fourteen.

Tyler: Same age as the King, officer.

Collector: I'll have to make sure, though.

Tyler: If you must.

[**The Collector** motions **The Daughter** over. He pulls the waistband of her skirt open. **The Daughter** slaps his face.]

Collector: Hold her!

[**The Daughter** tries to run away. **The Sergeant** catches her and pins her arms behind her, dropping his pike. **The Collector** approaches her cautiously.]

Collector: Now then.

[He pulls her waistband open. **The Daughter** knees him in the balls. **The Sergeant** throws her to the ground. **The Daughter** struggles. **The Parents** don't move. **The Collector** sits astride the girl and pulls her waistband open. He reaches down to feel for pubic hair. **John Tyler** kicks **The Collector** in the head and breaks his neck. **The Wife** grabs hold of the Sergeant's pike. **The Sergeant** runs off. **Abel Ker** comes in.]

Ker: Well well, John.

Tyler: He tried to finger her.

Ker: Happening everywhere.

Tyler: I've never struck a man before in my life, Abel Ker.

Ker: If the law's wrong, there's no sin in being an outlaw. The men of Erith have done me proud. We burned the monastery and every scrap of legal paper in it. The monks'll never wave that in our faces again. I was coming to ask you if you'd changed your mind.

Tyler: It was changed for me.

Ker: We found friends over the river, John, like I said. All Essex from Barking to Colchester is with us. We're joining Robert Cave and marching to Rochester. Will you come now?

Tyler: All I've done is defend my home. I don't want to destroy another man's home just because he's my enemy.

Ker: But if he can come into yours, John!

Tyler: That's his evil, not mine.

Ker: You're not pure, John. Even the Church says there are sins of omission, and they should know. To defend your home and your family you must attack those who threaten them.

Tyler: I haven't said I won't come.

Ker: You're a wise man, John. And you're gentle. If you come, others like you will follow. All we say is: no King but Richard. Is that right or wrong?

Tyler: That's right.

Ker: And will that happen with John of Gaunt, Richard Lyons and the others unless we fight for it?

Tyler: I don't know.

Ker: I'll tell you then: it won't.

Tyler: We can ask first. There's no reason to snatch what might be freely given.

Ker: Of course we'll ask first. We're not like them. Come on. We'll dump this in the river.

[They all go off. The drumbeat sounds again. **Someone** sings the fourth verse of 'The Yorkshire Partisans':]

And on that purpose yet we stand
whoso do us any wrong
in whate'er place it fall
yet he might as well
as I have flesh and soul
do against us all.

[As the song finishes, **Someone** announces:]

6th June: Rochester.
The rebel leader Robert Cave interviews Sir John Newton, Governor of Rochester Jail.

[A group of **Rebels,** led by **Robert Cave,** and including **A Citizen of Gravesend** and **Robert Belling,** bring on **Sir John Newton,** whose hands and feet are tied.]

Cave: Now then, Sir John, we've had good sport this day. The people of Rochester have been more than generous. They've fed us and given us room to rest. And we needed that, for we've come a long way to see you and the contents of your jail. Now we're going to perform a little magic with you, Sir John. We're going to turn your criminals into people. See how well you know your people, Sir John. Do you know the game 'Hoodman's Blind'?

[**One of the Rebels** blindfolds **Newton.** He is made to kneel with his hands stretched out behind him.]

37

Cave: Who's this, Sir John?

[**The First Prisoner** swipes **Newton**'s hands.]

Newton: I don't know.

Cave: Tell him, Will.

Prisoner 1: Will Carpenter. I charged my lord nine pence for three days' work repairing his wheat barn. It was four days after Michaelmas, and by the Statute I should have charged less. I didn't know that, though, till the justice came. Then my lord took his nine pence back.

Cave: Next!

[**Second Prisoner** swipes **Newton**'s hands.]

Cave: Who was that, Sir John?

Newton: I don't know.

Cave: You don't know your people very well, Sir John. You locked them up, you ought to know what they did. Tell him, John.

Prisoner 2: John Fuller. I was hired in secret by my lord's neighbour and offered a penny more per day than the Statute rate. I served three months. My lord's neighbour goes free.

Cave: Next!

[**Third Prisoner** swipes **Newton**'s hands.]

Cave: Well?

Newton: I don't know.

Prisoner 3: Robert Belling. After I had lived a year and a half in Gravesend, my former master Simon Burley reclaimed me as his serf and brought me to Rochester Jail.

Cave: They sound like criminals to you, Sir John?

Newton: They're thieves and murderers by law.

Cave: There'll be new laws, Sir John. Once the King hears how his commons have been treated. What will that make you?

Newton: I can only do my duty.

Cave: What is your duty?

To serve my King.

Cave: But the King will be on our side. You'll see. Can we have a murderer, please?

[**Fourth Prisoner** swipes **Newton**'s hands.]

Cave: Who was that?

Newton: I don't know.

Cave: Tell him, Ralph.

Prisoner 4: Ralph Dunning. I refused to buy ale from my lord's hayward, but went to the next village where they charged a fair price.

Our hayward caught me and threatened to have me seized.
I cleaved his head open with an axe.
Cave: Any thieves?

[**Fifth Prisoner** swipes **Newton**'s hands.]

Newton: I don't know.
Prisoner 5: Roger Cote. I shovelled up dung from the oxen in the street of our vill, to fertilise my strip. By law even that shit was my lord's.
Cave: Are those thieves and murderers, Sir John?
Newton: Every one of them was put in prison for an offence against the Crown.
Cave: We've got your children, Sir John, remember that. Now then, there's something else I have to ask you. We want someone we can call our leader. If people know you opened your jail to us and see you ahead of us as we march, they'll know our friends aren't really criminals and they'll feel better towards us. We want you to lead us into Maidstone, Sir John.
Newton: No.
Cave: Then we'll kill your children.

[Pause.]

Newton: Yes.
Cave: [Reads a letter] 'Jack Trueman doth you to understand that falseness and guile have reigned too long and truth hath been set under a lock and falseness reigneth in every flock. But with right and with might with skill and with will and skill before will and right before might then goeth our mill all right.'

John Ball said when they put him in Maidstone Jail that 20,000 men would soon come to release him. Tomorrow we'll prove him right.

[**A Citizen of Gravesend** steps forward.]

Gravesend: Robert Cave, the men of Gravesend shan't come to Maidstone. We came for Robert Belling. Now we've got him, we'll go home and live as before.
Cave: Who is your true lord?
Gravesend: King Richard and The True Commons.
Cave: The True Commons of Essex and Kent have saved you three hundred pounds today. They need your help now as

	before. Don't you feel you owe them your support?
Gravesend:	We've pledged our support. For countrymen June is no busy month. For us in the towns there's always work to be done. We want to go back to our work and our homes.
Cave:	One battle and you think you've won!
Gravesend:	There'll be food and shelter for the commons if they come back through Gravesend.
Cave:	Your arm is more use to us than your sympathy. But if you must go back, spread the word as you go. John Legge was turned back from Canterbury yesterday. There's news at every crossroads.

[**The Gravesend Citizen** and **Belling** go. **The Others** take the blindfold from **Newton** and untie him.]

| **Cave:** | Lead on, Sir John. Maidstone Jail. You know the way? |

[They go off. The drumbeat sounds. **Someone** sings the last verse of 'The Yorkshire Partisans'.]

| **John Ball:** | For unkind we were |

if we suffered less or more
any villain's teasing
but it were quit and double again
and accord and be full fayne
to bide our direction.

[As the song finishes, **John Ball** comes on. He carries the head of a nobleman on a spear. **Someone** announces:]

7th June: John Ball is released from Maidstone Jail

This is the head of a man who decided to place himself above other men. When you came to the city of Maidstone, my brothers, this man refused to join you. He refused to give up his wealth and possessions to the common good. He wished to remain aloof. Now he is aloft. No man shall be above another in station. No man shall command without the other's assent. St Paul says: 'The body is one, though it hath many members. And by one spirit are we baptised, whether bond or free. And those members which we think less honourable, upon those shall we bestow more abundant honour, so that there shall be no schism in the body, but that the members shall have the same care one for another. And if one member suffer, all the members suffer with it. Or if one member be honoured, all the members rejoice with it.' [He points to the head.] But a head that keeps apart from the body finishes like this one — detached. His shame, our

40

shame. You are the body, my brothers. Yours are the legs that have marched from Erith, Barking, Dartford, Brentwood, Waltham, Romney Marsh, Lydd and Malling. Yours are the arms that have fought soldiers' pikes, knights' swords, nobles' armies. You are many; many thousand. Much lies ahead of you. The road is open to Canterbury, where the rotting head of the church has its pillow. The road is open to London, where maggots surround the fresh young head of King Richard the Second. Now we are together, we must keep together and move swiftly. 'And the eye cannot say to the hand, I have no need of thee; nor again the head to the feet, I have no need of you.' But if men must have a head to know the body lives, then we too must have a head. But a head that serves its body. Only one King, only one leader. For more than one will divide us and send our arms and legs, our toes and our fingers spinning in all directions. It must be a wise head, but it must know you. It must teach us to march, but it must speak as you do. Because this afternoon we choose not only a head, but a voice for it to speak with. The voice of our body. Your voice. Choose wisely and choose well.

[He goes off. Drumbeat. **Someone** announces:]

The Commons chose Wat Tyler
10th June, Canterbury Cathedral, Wat Tyler and Jack Straw

[Below **Monks** come on singing a chant. **Wat Tyler** appears to one side. When **The Monks** are quiet, **Jack Straw** comes on with **The Mayor of Canterbury.**]

Straw: Wat, I'd like you to meet the Mayor of Canterbury.
Tyler: How d'you do.
Straw: He accepted our programme, swore his loyalty to The True Commons and broke open a barrel in the town hall for us.
Tyler: Good of you.
Mayor: My pleasure.
Straw: The town's put out the flags for us, Wat, co-operated all round. People are catching on.
Tyler: Good.

[Pause.]

Straw: Going in?
Tyler: I've got to tell them.
Straw: Think He'll be in there?
Tyler: Who, God?
Straw: The Archbishop.

41

Tyler: In London. With the other turds.

Straw: He wasn't home when we called. You should've seen it. Italian furniture, French hangings, Dutch bedspreads, the lot.

Tyler: We'll show him the bill in London.

Straw: Not that we didn't work it over. [He makes a slitting noise.]

Tyler: You burnt the scrolls, though.

Straw: Every record in the place. I saved you some ashes. [He pull ashes from his pocket.] Present.

[He grins, holds them up, pours them into **Tyler's** hand.]

Straw: We let everyone burn the roll he was personally entered on. Took time, but worth it. Makes it real for people.

Tyler: As long as it is.

Straw: It's a start.

Tyler: I'm going in.

Straw: Good luck.

Tyler: It's a cathedral. A bunch of monks. Think they're going to put a spell on me?

Straw: They're saying Mass.

Tyler: Perhaps they need to.

Straw: See you later.

[Down below **The Monks** kneel. **Tyler** comes in, on the balcony.]

Tyler: All right, listen here!

[The music stops. **The Monks** stand and turn.]

Tyler: The Commons of England came into this town today and put right much that was wrong. Your Archbishop, Thomas Sudbury, will be beheaded for his evil misgovernment of the King's Treasury, as will all traitors. So look to it you choose a new archbishop pleasing to The True Commons. For in future there will be only one King and only one Bishop, and all others will be equal. The goods of the Church will be returned to the people. Its priests, bishops and monks will be like other men. Those who protest will be executed and their goods burned, as happened here today. You stand warned. God be with you.

[He goes out. **The Monks,** faceless as ever, go off as if nothing had happened. Drumbeat. **Someone** announces:]

11th June: The main road from Canterbury to London

[**Two Peasants** stand with a banner.]

42

First: Why can't we go with the rest? I never been to London. I don't see the point.

Second: All the pilgrims in and out of Canterbury come past here. Spread the word to them, we're doing a good job.

First: Where are they all then? We been here two hours and I ain't seen a soul.

Second: It's early yet. — Here are.

First: Where?

Second: There, look.

First: Just the one?

Second: Who'll ask him?

First: Me.

Second: Go on then.

[**First** steps forward to meet the man. It is **William Langland**.]

First: Stop!

Langland: Who are you?

First: My name's John Hermare of Essex. Who are you? With whom do you hold?

Langland: My name's William Langland. I hold with myself.

First: You should say: 'With King Richard and The True Commons'.

Langland: Why? What I do is hard enough.

Second: The Commons are rising, that's why. Where'd you come from?

Langland: Cornhill. In London.

Second: What you do?

Langland: I'm a scholar. I was trained in the Church, but now I write verse.

First: That's not much use.

Langland: Oh I don't know. I'm read quite widely. I travel a lot.

Second: Bit shabby for a poet.

Langland: Not all poets are courtiers. I was born a peasant and I'm no richer now.

First: Where you going?

Langland: Canterbury.

Second: Pious, are you?

Langland: I serve no man above God.

Second: If you get around so much, you can help us. When you go back, spread the word through Surrey. The True Commons are marching. Today they were in Canterbury, in two days London.

Langland: Are you going with them?

First: We hope so.

Langland: Then be careful.

When the Cat is a Kitten
the Court is full of Rats.
It's hard not to get smitten
by the claws of Fat Cats.
But you know a Fat Cat if one you see,
while a Rat, my friends, is just a fatter You and Me.
Cats and Mice will play the same game,
but Rats get greedy when they're no longer tame.
No Mouse becomes a Cat,
but it's easier to see that
than a Mouse who's got fat
and become a Fat Rat.

First: Eh?

Second: We'll be careful.

First: He's off his head!

Langland: I will go back through Surrey. Mice who show their teeth don't attract me. But I'll tell the others to keep their tails from getting trodden on, and to watch for Fat Rats.

[He goes.]

First: This job's dangerous. They didn't tell us there were madmen loose on the road.

Second: Look at that, will you?

[From the opposite direction **The Queen Mother** comes on, carried on an ornate sedan chair by **Two Soldiers.**]

First: Stop! With whom do you hold?

[**The Soldiers** put the chair down and draw their swords.]

Soldier 1: Who are you? Declare yourselves!

First: We're ... er ... agents of King Richard and The True Commons.

Soldier 1: So?

[**First** turns to second for help.]

Second: We're stopping everyone on this road to tell them the Commons are rising and will soon be in London. Everyone is called upon to spread the word, take up arms and join us.

Soldier 2: Look, we've got the Queen Mother on here.

Second: Oh.

Q. Mother: [pulls back a curtain] What's going on here?

Soldier 1: We know what's going on in Canterbury. We've just come from there. That's why she's off back to London. We've got to get a move on or we'll be right in the shit.

First: Slave!

44

Soldier 2: Watch it!

Second: Look, the word's going round London too. People are putting their heads together. In two days we'll be in London and there'll be no stopping us. Tell your friends. We'll see you there. Have a drink together.

Soldier 2: If you can make London in two days' marching, you'll deserve a drink.

[**The Soldiers** pick up the chair.]

Second: Cheers.

Q. Mother: What was all that about?

Soldier: They wanted the road to Malling, Ma'am. I put 'em right. I'll save my breath now, Ma'am, with your permission. We're a bit behind.

[**The Queen Mother** retires behind her curtain. **The First Peasant** is peeing in a ditch. The Second Peasant claps him on the shoulder.]

Second: Come on, food.

First: Oi, careful!

[They go off. Drumbeat. **Someone** announces:]

12th June, late evening: Blackheath

[**Alan Threader** and **John Stackpole,** rebel leaders, come on and throw themselves down, exhausted.]

Threader: I'm all in.

Stackpole: We made it, though.

[**Wat Tyler** comes on.]

Tyler: Have you seen? Other side of the river?

[They stand and **Tyler** takes them to a raised spot, one side of the stage.]

Stackpole: Jesus!

Threader: Must be a good five hundred.

Tyler: 30,000.

Stackpole: Really?

Tyler: Jack Straw's men. The whole of Essex. We're as many this side.

Stackpole: They won't stop us now.

Threader: That London? [He points.]

Tyler: Yeh.

Threader: That's [London] no match for that [Straw's men].

Tyler: It looks smaller because it's further away.

45

Stackpole: Londoners!

Tyler: Lot of 'em started off in the country, same as us. They're as hard off as we are. It's no easier if you're poor.

Threader: You can't trust 'em though.

Tyler: We don't have to. We never trusted Maidstone or Rocheste or Canterbury. Just walked in. There's always more poor than rich. You soon make friends.

Stackpole: Any more work tonight?

Tyler: This side of the river there's the Marshalsea, Lambeth. Statute-breakers' prison. And Archbishop Sudbury's Palace Friends of ours in the prison. We may need them tomorro at London Bridge.

Stackpole: We got time now?

Tyler: If you like.

Stackpole: Come on, Alan.

[**Threader** and **Stackpole** get ready to go.]

Threader: The men ain't eaten, Wat.

Stackpole: Tomorrow they can stuff their faces. The victuallers are for us Is that right Wat?

Tyler: Here's an alderman coming now. Ask him.

Stackpole: No thanks.

[**John Horn** comes on.]

Horn: Wat Tyler?

Tyler: Yes.

Horn: I'm Alderman Horn.

[They shake hands. **Threader** and **Stackpole** make to go.

Tyler: Where you going?

Threader: Marshalsea. Then the Palace if we've got time.

Stackpole: We'll let you know what happens.

Tyler: See you later.

[They go.]

Horn: It wasn't easy getting here. I was sent with two others. I had to lose them. Mayor Walworth sent us in fact to war you not to enter the city.

Tyler: If it's going to be hard, we may not. Some of our people are very tired. No-one's eaten today. Some've been on the road ten days. They get homesick.

Horn: You must go in, though. Who will the other two speak to?

Tyler: Tom Hawk, John Sterling, there's any number of 'leaders'. We'll sit late tonight and talk it over.

Horn: We'll feed you tomorrow. You can sleep on beds, under roofs. We'll lay it on. It's a rich city, rich pickings. There's a lot at stake.

Tyler: It's different for you than us, though.

Horn: How?

Tyler: We shan't be used, John Horn. We'll use you first.

Horn: Of course. That's what I'm here for. There's a man called Sibley holds London Bridge. Walter Sibley, a colleague. [He makes a rocking motion with his hand.] You know? But flexible. William Tonge has Aldgate. The same. [He takes out a map.]

Tyler: If we feel like it.

Horn: But you must strike now. Before they realise.

Tyler: One way in each for Kent and Essex?

Horn: There's only the Bridge to the South. Aldersgate's another to the North.

Tyler: If we come, we'll come from all sides. Two ways in are too easy to block. Whatever you can give us we'll use, and more. But thank-you for your work. You'd better get back to Mister Walworth.

Horn: I'll tell him you're not coming. You're too tired.

Tyler: That we are.

Horn: I can take men with me. The leaders you mentioned. To stir support inside.

Tyler: Ask them.

Horn: I could feed them.

Tyler: They'd be glad of that.

[**Sterling, Hawk, Newman** and **De La Warde** come on.]

Sterling: Wat, we've had two London aldermen turn up.

[They see **Horn.**]

Tyler: This is the third. John Horn. Says the gates'll be open tomorrow. Food and rest inside.

Horn: If you come back into London with me tonight, I can show you.

[**The Four** look at **Tyler.**]

Tyler: If you go in now, and we decide not to go in tomorrow, you could be stuck there. And if we do decide to go in, we'll need your support at London Bridge tomorrow. — Can you leave us, Mr Horn? We'll have to discuss this on our own.

[**John Horn** goes.]

Hawk: Who says we're not going in tomorrow?

Tyler: No-one.

Warde: We've got to keep him and his kind in doubt, that all. Once we're inside, the apprentices, the journeymen, and the small tradesmen will all be on our side, like before. But his kind you can't count on.

Sterling: Right. The victuallers are for us now, because they see us as allies against John of Gaunt.

Tyler: But if Mayor Walworth plays a heavy hand to defend his city, our present friends could turn face about. Go and drink Alderman Horn's wine by all means, sleep with his girls on down, but don't let on.

Sterling: We'll need at least one of us this side tonight. There's Mayor Walworth's brothels want smashing.

Tyler: By push of 30,000 starved and fagged-out loins, if necessary.

Newman: You'd be getting it free.

Warde: That sounds like me.

[They laugh.]

Hawk: What about the message to the King? We ought to decide that first.

Tyler: Right. What's it to be?

[Pause.]

Hawk: Hang Hobb the Robber.

Newman: The Archbishop.

Sterling: Hang Bealknap, John Legge, Richard Lyons, the whole bunch.

Hawk: Burn the city.

Warde: Hang the King.

[Pause.]

Newman: What?

Warde: You never thought about it?

Newman: No!

Warde: Why spare him? He's no more a peasant than the rest.

Tyler: He's not God.

Hawk: Kill him, though, and there's nothing.

[Pause.]

Hawk: No country without the King. Just a load of people.

Sterling: And John of Gaunt.

Warde: There's you and me.

Newman: What can we do without the King?

Warde: We got this far, didn't we?

48

Hawk: No father, no family. No shepherd, no sheep. If we kill the King, then what?

Tyler: We sit down like this and see.

Sterling: If people know there's a King, they know there's a country. The King's young. If we tell him our grievances, he may still be fair. If we name the traitors, we can divide him from them. With the King on our side we can take him all over England with us, people will know us through him, and his power will be our power.

Tyler: When I was a soldier in France, I served under Richard Lyons. There was a mutiny, and I had Lyons' throat under the point of my sword. But I spared him, because I thought if I killed him, no-one woud pay us the wages. A week later those of us who mutinied were on half pay and bread and water. I don't believe in half measures.

Sterling: But Wat, people don't know what we stand for yet. If we declare ourselves by killing the King, we'll lose more friends than we make. With no law in the land each man will be afraid of his neighbour and strike out blindly to protect himself. In a fight like that it's the strong who win. And we aren't the strong. That's why we came here.

Warde: We're not weak now, John! Look at us! We can make new law, our own law.

Newman: We'd have John of Gaunt instead of Richard. That's even worse.

Hawk: With his army too. We can't risk that.

[Pause. It's three against two.]

Warde: I think it's the wrong decision.

Tyler: So do I.

Sterling: We can take the King later. If he turns against us.

Tyler: All right. Make a list of the traitors, Robert. Tom, bring John Newton.

[**Hawk** goes.]

Sterling: There must be one message, Wat, not several.

Newman: He must come to us, not us to him.

Warde: John Ball for Archbishop.

Tyler: Yes. We must make him see those about him are corrupt. A boy sees contradiction more clearly than a man.

[**Hawk** returns with **Newton.**]

Tyler: We want you to go to the King, Sir John. Tell him this: The country has been badly governed. There are people of our kind oppressed by the Church or arrogant lords, and they are starving. The tax has helped no-one. If the King will meet us here, we'll state our grievances in full. We have a list . . .

[He turns to **De La Warde**.]

Warde: Fifteen names, off-hand. All traitors.
Tyler: We want their heads. Take this list and tell the King. He'll come to no harm. All we've done and will do is for him and his honour. A King that honours his people is honoured by his people. Only one King, only one Bishop. No Johns for King. King Richard and The True Commons, all equal under one head. And we will dispatch the traitors. We must have an answer. We hold your children. [He turns to the others.] Is that all?
Sterling: Yes.
Tyler: Do you understand your message, John Newton?
Newton: Yes.
Tyler: Find the King for us then. You've behaved well here.
Warde: Come on.

[**Warde** takes **Newton** off.]

Tyler: Now. For you three, London. Keep an eye open for friends. Stir them, let them know. We need men at London Bridge and Aldgate tomorrow morning. As for John Horn, take all he offers and restore your strength. There'll be more fun tomorrow. But he mustn't know that. For sure.
Sterling: Shall a boat go across to Jack Straw's men?
Tyler: Yes. Aldgate will be open, tell him. Aldersgate might. Lunch at the Savoy.

[**Sterling** claps **Wat** on the shoulder. They leave. **Wat** settles down comfortably for the night. **Warde** returns.]

Warde: I've found one or two with enough left in 'em for Walworth's brothels. They say the women there are all Flemish.
Tyler: Have a Dutch girl for me, then.

[**Tyler** goes to sleep. **Warde** goes off. **Someone** announces:]

The same night: in the Tower of London

[On the gallery, **The Queen Mother, Richard, Sudbury, Salisbury, Hales** and **Walworth** come on.]

Q. Mother: I feel much safer here, dear.
Richard: It must have been awful for you, mother.
Q. Mother: Held up on the open road! My heart was in my boots.
Sudbury: You were lucky to get away.

50

Q. Mother: My guard was no help. They stood chatting.

Hales: We'll have them executed.

Q. Mother: Thank goodness for four strong walls.

Richard: The Tower is certainly much better than Westminster, isn't it. But it does seem rather crowded.

Walworth: With Your Majesty's permission, half the aristocracy of the home counties has come here for safety.

Salisbury: Several hundred of 'em.

Walworth: Well, a good hundred and fifty. The other half are in the woods, living on acorns and berries like outlaws. There's a messenger from the rebels outside, Your Majesty. He has the latest news.

Richard: We ought to see him, oughtn't we?

Hales: Yes.

[**Walworth** off to bring **Newton.**]

Richard: Why does this have to happen now, uncle?

Salisbury: Probably because John's away.

Richard: Would he know how to deal with it?

Salisbury: He'd deal with it. I don't know if he'd be right.

[**Walworth** returns with **Newton** who flings himself at **Richard**'s feet.]

Newton: Your Majesty, I am the rebels' prisoner. They forced me to come as their messenger.

Salisbury: We know that. Get up, man.

Richard: Sir John, say what you will. We hold you excused.

Newton: Sir, the commons of your realm desire you to come and speak with them on Blackheath. You need have no fear of your person, for they hold and will hold you for their King. They say they will show you diverse things which you must take heed of, and they have given me a list of names. Of traitors, as they call them. These they will behead.

[He hands **Richard** the list. **Richard** reads.]

Richard: They will have none but me?

Newton: None named John, sir.

[**Richard** looks up at **Hales** and **Sudbury.**]

Richard: Robert, Simon, they want your heads.

Sudbury: Your Majesty, you must not go to Blackheath. I think it best if you retire to Windsor.

Richard: We've only just come from there. Besides I want to go. They've invited me.

Sudbury: They'll kill us all.

51

Salisbury: Your Majesty, Audacitee may be a fashionable virtue, bu if these rebels are successful, it will be all over with us and Engand will be as a desert. You must protect yourself.

Richard: Oh I shall. Don't worry.

Newton: Sir, will you give me an answer to appease them? So that they may know in fact I have spoken to you. They hold my children in hostage. I'm afraid they may kill them otherwise.

Hales: The only answer is to put them down. Put them in their pla

Salisbury: There's more than 50,000 of them out there. Can you lay hands on as many again to put them down?

Hales: The situation's ridiculous. Out of hand. Who do they think they are?

Richard: My commons. They've always said so. Shall I go tomorrow

Salisbury: If you wish to.

Richard: By boat. That'll be fun. Tell them that, Sir John.

Newton: Thank-you, sir.

[He goes. **The Lords** are silent.]

Richard: I'm hungry.

[He goes off. **The Queen Mother** follows. **Sudbury** takes off his chain (The Great Seal) and gives it to **Salisbury.**]

Sudbury: I've had enough. Give him that tomorrow. I'm retiring to the country. Don't try to stop me.

Salisbury: I shan't stop you. But which road were you thinking of taking?

Sudbury: I'll cross that hurdle when I come to it. Let's eat.

[He goes off. **The Others** follow. **Walworth,** last, makes sure everything's left as it should be.
Someone announces:]

The next morning, 13th June: Blackheath

[**John Ball** comes on and stands on a raised place to give h early morning sermon. Below **Wat Tyler** wakes up.]

John Ball: 'When Adam delved and Eve span
Who was then the gentleman?'
From the beginning all men were made alike by nature.
Bondage and servitude were brought in by the oppression
of evil men against the will of God. For if it had pleased
God to have made bondsmen, would he not have appointed
from the beginning of the world who would be slave and
who lord? Now is the time given by God, if you choose, to
lay aside bondage and enjoy that long wished-for liberty.

52

So be wise, and like a good husbandman that tills his ground, do not shirk to cut away all noisome weeds that are accustomed to grow and oppress the fruit.

First the Archbishop and all those called great men of the kingdom. After, lawyers and justices who you know to be hurtful to the commons. Dispatch them out of the land, for so will you purchase safety for yourselves hereafter if, the great men being taken away, there remains among you equal liberty, all one nobility, and like authority and power. Amen.

[**King Richard**, **Salisbury**, **Sudbury**, **Hales** and **Walworth** come on aboard a barge.]

Salisbury: My God!
Hales: Look at them!

[A large shout goes up. The chant 'Hobb the Robber, Hobb the Robber' mingles with it.]

Salisbury: Disgusting.
Richard: Look, they've got Sir John with them. Tied up. They're waving a sword over his head. It's as well we came.
Sudbury: All right, we've come, they've seen us, now let's go back for God's sake!
Richard: Archbishop!
Sudbury: I'm sorry, but I'm very frightened.
Richard: Are we going to land?
Salisbury: Row up and down a bit. That's best. Try and get the feel of them.
Richard: Perhaps I should ask them what they want.
Hales: Is that wise?
Richard: [stands up suddenly and rocks the boat] Commons of England! I have come to speak with you as you desired. What is it you want?
Voice: You come aland, boy, we'll show you what we lack!
Salisbury: [standing] Gentlemen, you are not in a fit condition, neither are you properly dressed for a King to talk to. — They're all drunk. Turn her about. Disgusting.

[The barge turns about.]

Sudbury: Thank God for that.
Richard: There are a lot of them.
Salisbury: One should never commit oneself to a situation like that, Your Majesty. You were surrounded. They could have done with you what they liked.
Richard: I can't run away from them for ever, uncle.

Salisbury: Our time will come, Richard. Something's bound to happen. They might even break up of their own accord. Aren't I right, Walworth?

Walworth: I hope so, sir.

[**Sudbury** vomits.]

Richard: Oh, Archbishop!

Sudbury: I don't know why you made me come.

Hales: Vicious brutes, that's all they are.

[The Royal Barge disappears, **Someone** announces:]

13th June, midday:
Geoffrey Chaucer's room over Aldgate

[**Geoffrey Chaucer** comes on the balcony. He is working on 'Canterbury Tales'. He takes a swig of wine, then reads:]

Chaucer: 'Now will I turn to my tale again
This poor widow and eek her daughters two
Heard the hens cry and maken woe
And out of doors started they anon
And saw the fox towards the grove gone
And bare upon his back their cock away
And cryden: 'Out harrow and wail away!
Ha-ha, the fox!' And after him they ran
And eek with sticks many another man.'

[He takes another nip of wine and continues.]

'And eek with sticks many another man.
Ran sows and calf and eek the very hogs
So were they feared for barking of the dogs
And shouting of the men and women eek
They ran so they thought their hearts would break.'

[Very quietly, the noise of the mob advancing on Aldgate is heard. **Chaucer** takes another nip, repeats his last line, then writes:]

'They ran so they thought their hearts would break.
The geese for fear flew over the trees
Out of the hive came a swarm of bees
So hideous was the noise . . . '

[He stops rigid, hearing the distant roar of **The Rebels**. It grows. Shouts are heard very near. Chants of 'Jack Straw Jack Straw!' **Chaucer** drops his glass. In a cold sweat, he sits down. **The Rebels** roar on through Aldgate, drinking,

shouting somersaulting, fighting, making love. **Chaucer** is
under the table. He looks out. **A Straggler** comes on.]

Straggler: Wait for me!

[**Chaucer** hides again. When the noise has passed, he
brushes himself down, pours a drink, regains his composure.
Confident again, he writes:]

Chaucer: 'So hideous was the noise, a Benedicitee!
Certainly Jack Straw and his many
Nay never made shouts half so shrill
When that they would any Fleming kill'
— That'll go down well —
'As that day was made upon the fox.'

[He leers outrageously, dries his paper, then goes. **The
Rebels'** roar begins to swell up again. **Someone** announces:]

13th June, afternoon:
The Savoy Palace

[The announcement is nearly drowned by **The Rebels,**
who are everywhere. Barrels are rolled in and wine is drunk.
People bring in clothes, cloths, coverlets, curtains and
drapings, rip them up and throw them on the cart to be
burned. The cart is wheeled off. Smoke and a red glow are
glimpsed off-stage. **A Rebel with an 'F'** on his forehead,
carrying a longbow and arrows, stands on a platform.]

Rebel 'F': John of Gaunt, it was you brought in the first poll tax!
This place, the cellar of your Palace of Savoy, was built
over labourers' backs for foundations! It's a sign to us, like
the 'F' on my forehead: False! Traitor! It stands for fixed
wages, high prices and high rents! [He picks up an expensive
piece of cloth.] This is three months' ploughing! [He tears
the cloth through. He picks up a small ornate piece of
furniture.] This is John Ball's three terms in Maidstone Jail!
[He smashes it. He picks up a ring with jewels.] The three
jewels in this ring are your three poll taxes!

[He crushes it underfoot. **Two Rebels** run on with an
expensive-looking short jacket.]

Look, a 'jakke', a 'jakke'! Jack's 'jakke'!

Rebel 3: Nail it to the wall. We'll have some target practice.

[They pin the jacket to the wall. **Rebel with 'F' on his
forehead** begins shooting at it. **Rebel 2** comes in with a
headboard covered in ornate heraldry. **Mrs Chaucer** follows.]

55

Mrs. Chaucer: Don't please! That's worth a thousand pounds!

> [A solitary incredulous whistle. **Rebel 2** throws it on the car which is wheeled off to hoots and cheers. A fight breaks out between two drunken rebels.]

Rebel 3: We was here first, mate.

Rebel 4: We was!

Rebel 3: Essex, mate.

Rebel 4: Kent.

Rebel 3: Come off it, the pair of you. The London mob was in here, pissed up to the eyeballs while you were still knocking on the back door.

Rebel 4: Don't you fucking start.

Rebel 3: Kids himself, don't he.

Rebel 5: You'd do better punching up a few of them Flemmies. It's them pinching all the good jobs, you know.

Rebel 3: Don't tell me what I already know, son.

Rebel 5: Bleeding yokels. One mug of decent ale and you're like wild animals.

Rebel 3: London ponce!

Rebel 4: Here, shh!

> [**Tyler** and **Straw** have come in. They are eating. **Tyler** goes to the platform to make an announcement.]

Straw: Food all right?

Tyler: I invited Y O U. I spilt blood in France for John of Gaunt's poultry. [He gets up on the platform.] N O - O N E ! No-one on pain to lose his head shall convert to his own use anything found in this cellar. All plates and vessels of gold and silver shall be broken into small pieces and thrown into the Thames. Clothes of silk and velvet shall be torn. Rings and ornaments set with precious stones shall be ground in mortars so they're of no use. We do not wish to be thieves.

> [He gets down.]

Straw: [Offering **Tyler** wine.] Wash it down?

Tyler: Let's go upstairs.

> [They go.]

Rebel 4: You heard him.

Rebel 2: What?

Rebel 4: No nicking things for yourself.

Rebel 2: What things?

Rebel 3: That plate you got stuffed up your shirt.

Rebel 2: What plate?

Rebel 4: Come on.

[**Rebels 3** and **4** pounce on **Rebel 2** and take away a silver plate.]

Rebel 3: It's death, son.

Rebel 2: Oh come on, it's only a plate.

Rebel 3: You don't want people to think we're rough. They will anyway, you know that.

Rebel 4: Chuck him on the fire.

Rebel 2: No!

[**Rebels 3** and **4** bundle **Rebel 2** towards the fire. **Rebel 2** struggles. They throw him off. A terrible scream. Silence. They come back.]

Rebel 3: Bastard bit me.

Rebel 4: It's not discipline if you don't mean it.

[**Thomas Farringdon** comes in. He sees the 'jakke', rips it from the wall and holds it up.]

Farringdon: So much for John of Gaunt! All that's left to do here is drink this cellar dry, and there'll be no satisfaction in that tomorrow, except a sore head. Twenty minutes from here is the Temple, property of Hobb the Robber, Treasurer of England, crawling with lawyers, their records and their rolls. All waiting to be burned. If you've got more than wine in your heads, follow me there!

[He goes. Several **Rebels** follow him. **Rebel 5** has found another barrel. He rolls it over to **Rebel 1.**]

Rebel 1: Not more. I couldn't manage it. Coming out faster than it's going in.

Rebel 5: 'Snot wine. 'Sheavier. Solid gold.

Rebel 1: Nah.

Rebel 5: Silver then. Feel.

Rebel 1: You reckon?

[He feels the weight of the barrel.]

Rebel 1: If it's not booze, it goes on the fire. No matter what.

Rebel 5: Easier said than done, mate.

[**Rebels 1** and **5** roll the barrel towards the fire. Huge explosion. Sound of falling debris. A thud against the door.]

Rebel 5: Whassat?

Rebel 1: Go and see.

Rebel 5: You.

Rebel 1: I said first.
Rebel 5: Yes.

[He goes. He can't get the door open.]

Rebel 5: Something blocking the door.
Rebel 1: What?

[He goes and tries the door.]

Rebel 1: No good. Any other doors?
Rebel 5: No.
Rebel 1: Fuck.
Rebel 5: We'll be stuck down here.
Rebel 1: Fuck.
Rebel 5: Trapped.
Rebel 1: We won't get out. They'll never think to look in the cellar.
Rebel 5: Something'll turn up.
Rebel 1: Yeh, we'll die.
Rebel 5: Must've been gunpowder.
Rebel 1: [Looking round at the barrels.] What a way to go, though

[They settle down to the wine.
Someone announces:]

14th June: The Tower and the meeting at Mile End

[**The Rebels** go off. On the balcony **Richard, Salisbury, Hales, Sudbury** and **Walworth** appear. Quiet, glow of flame

Richard: They're burning everything.
Hales: Particularly what belongs to me, it seems.
Sudbury: It's your own fault. You shouldn't have appropriated Thomas Farringdon's land. Now he's using the rebels to get at you.
Hales: I'm not the only one!
Sudbury: Hobb the Robber indeed!
Walworth: Your Majesty, if I may speak, we A L L of us stand to lose everything we care for.
Hales: He means his brothels.
Richard: Advise me what to do then.
Walworth: Sir, it's time these shoeless ruffians were taught a lesson. There's a lull in the rioting. Many of the rebels are asleep. My aldermen are in contact with several of the larger housholds within the city. If these could be persuaded to rally their private armies, we could ride through the city, putting down rebels wherever we found them.
Hales: It was your aldermen, Walworth, who let the bastards in in the first place.

Walworth: Three traitors out of twelve aldermen, Sir Robert, that's all.

Hales: I suppose it just happened that they were the three in charge of London Bridge, Aldgate and Aldersgate.

Walworth: Their treachery was supported by their own ingenuity, sir, not by my negligence. I had no reason to suppose they would renegue.

Salisbury: Forgive my saying this, Walworth, but you and your class are relatively new to the problems of power. We of the nobility have weathered centuries of cantankerousness from servants because we're cleverer. The serf looks to us for guidance and only rebels when he doesn't get it. If things appear to go well, that's enough for him. Brute force causes retaliation. Conciliation, appeasement, compromise, these things have worked in the favour of the British aristocracy for years. There are fifty thousand rebels scattered around this city. If we sally forth now, by midday they'll be at our throats again. If we start something we can't finish, we and our heirs shall be disinherited for ever. My suggestion is, play friendly. Get them all in one place where you can see them and agree to everything they ask. Their demands will be woolly, and anything too painful can be revoked when convenient later. We may go a bit off course now, but if we're still steering, we can always pull her back. I suggest you go out on the balcony, Mr Walworth, and read out a proclamation to the effect that they should all put their grievances in writing and go home. And we'll see they're looked into. We've been doing that on the manor for centuries.

Richard: Could you write this proclamation for me, uncle?

Salisbury: Of course, Richard. [He writes the proclamation.]

Sudbury: [To **Hales**.] You know what they'll request, don't you. Your head and mine. I'm going.

Hales: Again?

[**Sudbury** goes out.]

Richard: What happened to that food we sent for?

Walworth: The rebels have got it, Your Majesty. Six hundred of them blocking all entries to the Tower. They intercepted your food and took it for themselves. I can't see Lord Simon getting beyond the back door.

[Below.]

Woman: Oi, what you doing? 'Ere, it's the Archbishop!

Rebel 1: Come on, lads!

Woman: Too late. He's seen you. Gone back in.

[**Salisbury** hands **Walworth** the proclamation. **Walworth** reads it to the **Rebels** below.]

Walworth: 'The King thanks his good commons for their loyalty and pardons all their illegal offences, but he wishes everyone to return home and set down his grievances in writing and send them to him. With the aid of his good lords and loya council he will then provide such remedy as will be profitab to himself, his commons, and the whole realm.'

[**Jack Straw,** below, spits. **Sudbury** returns above.]

Rebel 1: You're joking!

Rebel 2: What illegal offences?

Straw: We've not come this far to give you paper to tear up!

Rebel 3: You can do better than that, Dickie!

Straw: Watch yourselves! We'll be in there after the bunch of conniving prats who drew that up and we'll have their hair

Rebel 1: Yes!

[Shouts and laughter.]

Walworth: They won't accept it, Your Majesty.

Hales: So much for 300 years of aristocratic experience.

Salisbury: Appeasement is always better than brute force, Lord Hales.

Hales: Backed by brute force, Lord Salisbury, it's even better.

Salisbury: Obviously I can give you no more advice, your Majesty. The rebels are powerful and determined. Between them and us is a wall of knights, merchants and clergy who refuse to commit themselves. You know what the people want. They have addressed themselves to you throughout this affair. It's up to you to answer them.

Richard: It would be bad, wouldn't it, if they killed the Archbishop and Lord Hales?

[Silence.]

Salisbury: I shall leave at the first opportunity.

Richard: The rebels say they are my friends. You, Mr Walworth, say friends' armies are standing by.

[Pause.]

Richard: I shall go to them.

Walworth: Outside the city is best, sir . . .

[He breaks off. He has spoken out of turn.]

Richard: William Walworth, tell them I will meet them at Mile End. All of them. I will hear what they have to say and do my best to answer them.

[**Walworth** looks for confirmation from **The Lords.** No response. Their morale is at its lowest. He speaks to **The Commons:**]

Walworth: All persons within the walls of the City of London between the ages of fifteen and sixty, on pain of life and limb, shall proceed to Mile End, where the King will come in person to hear your grievances and answer them.

[He turns back. **Richard** stands there.]

Richard: Will anyone come with me?

[No response.]

Richard: Goodbye then.

[He goes.]

Hales: He's disowned us. They'll separate us and him.
Sudbury: Is the Tower guard strong?
Hales: Hand-picked men. But soldiers are commoners.
Salisbury: Obviously the King is growing up.

[He goes.]

Sudbury: Prayer, that's all that's left.
Hales: I'll join you.
Sudbury: Surely the chapel will be safe?

[**Hales** and **Sudbury** go. **Walworth** casts a quick eye round, as before, and goes. Below **Jack Straw,** with a group of **Rebels,** chats up **A Soldier** of the **Tower Guard.**]

Straw: You're more like us than you are them, aren't you?
Soldier: It's my job to guard this door.
Straw: Who for?
Soldier: The King, I suppose.
Straw: We stand for the King, though. 'With whom hold you?' — 'With King Richard and the True Commons.' That's us.
Soldier: He's in there, though, and you're out here.
Straw: How much d'you get a week?
Soldier: Four pence.
Straw: So do I. Shake.

[**The Soldier** doesn't.]

Straw: How much d'you think Walworth gets?

[No answer.]

Straw: Eh?

                       [No answer.]

Straw: D'you give or take orders?
Soldier: Take.
Straw: So do I. Shake.

                    [**The Soldier** doesn't.]

Straw: There's a lot of us, you know.
Soldier: I know. I've seen.
Straw: We'll see you all right. Don't worry. We'll need blokes like you to settle with the traitors.
Soldier: I thought you were the traitors.
Straw: You don't want to believe what they tell you in there. Glory, honour, duty, all that crap. You know whose side you're on when it comes down to it, don't you?
Soldier: The King's.
Straw: We been fighting the King's battles a fortnight. And we ain't got pikes like that either. He's coming to chat with us You'll see.

[The doors open and **Richard** comes out on a horse. The crowd applauds. **Richard** is rigid with fear. He looks straig ahead at first, succumbing eventually to a faint, awkward smile. He advances slowly. This part is silent. To show h fear and **The Rebels'** reverence. Once or twice **Rebels** can't control themselves and move forward to touch him. F first reaction is to shy away, but then he gets used to it, enjoys it, holds out his hand to be touched.]

Straw: He's on his own.
Farringdon: The rest are inside.

[**Thomas Farringdon** steps up to **Richard** and holds his horse still.]

Farringdon: Your Majesty, my name is Thomas Farringdon. That false traitor Robert Hales has falsely and fraudulently seized m inheritance. Do right justice in my case. Restore my tenements to me. Otherwise know that I am strong enough to secure entry for myself.
Richard: Thomas Farringdon, you shall have what is just. As shall everyone. Come to Mile End and there speak your grievanc

[**Richard** rides his horse on. **Farringdon** hesitates, then decides to rejoin **The Rebels** at the doors to the Tower.]

Straw: [to **Soldier**] That proof enough for you?

Soldier: I didn't see you.

[**The Rebels** enter the Tower. **Tyler** and others follow **Richard,** who continues his ride. From behind heavy church music. **Sudbury** and **Hales** are heard praying in Latin. A scream. **The Queen Mother** comes on to the balcony, pursued by **Rebel 1.**]

Rebel 1: Come on darling, give us a kiss.

[He plants a smacker on **The Queen Mother,** who faints. **Hales** comes on, chased by **Straw.**]

Rebel 1: Didn't know I had it in me.

[He picks up **The Queen** and carries her off.]

Straw: [to **Hales**] Give us a touch of your beard then, master.

[**Hales** stands rigid. **Straw** feels his face.]

Straw: Nice.

[**Farringdon** comes on.]

Farringdon: That's him! That's Hobb the Robber!

Straw: Fucking hell!

[He wipes his hand. They carry **Hales** off, struggling. Below, **Sudbury** is pushed on by **The Rebels.**]

Sudbury: I shan't run away. Better to die when it can no longer help to live. At no previous time in my life could I have died with a better conscience.

Rebel 2: Yeh, I bet.

[**Straw** bursts in.]

Straw: Where is he? The traitor. The exploiter.

Sudbury: I am the Archbishop, my son, and neither a traitor nor an exploiter.

Straw: Get over there.

[There is a platform.]

Sudbury: What is it you propose to do? What sin have I committed that you wish to kill me?

Rebel 2: Less of your lip and lie down.

Sudbury: Beware, my sons. If you kill me, your pastor, I have no doubt that for such a deed the Pope will lay an interdiction on all England.

Straw: Don't kid yourself. Lie down.

63

Sterling: The Pope's as big a villain as you are. Head up there.

    [**The Archbishop** lies so his head hangs from the platform away from the audience.]

Straw: Now!

    [**Sterling,** the executioner, swings. He does not sever the head.]

Sudbury: Agh! This is the hand of God!

    [We see **Sudbury's** fingers go up to his neck.]

Sterling: [panicky] Get your fingers out of it.

    [No reaction.]

Sterling: All right.

    [He swings again. The hand falls limp over the platform edge.]

Straw: Got his fingers an' all.

    [**Sterling** swings again.]

Rebel 2: Making heavy weather of that, John.

    [**Sterling** swings again. The head is off.]

Sterling: Jesus.

    [**The Rebels** cheer. **Rebel 2** picks up the head.]

Rebel 2: Messy job.

    [He fixes the head on a spear. **Sterling** vomits. **Straw** put Sudbury's mitre on the head.]

Straw: Don't forget this. So people know who he is.

    [**Rebel 1** picks something up.]

Rebel 1: I got a finger.

    [He pops it in his pocket. **Hales** is brought on struggling, by **Farringdon** and **Rebel 3**. **Hales** sees the Archbishop's corpse and breaks away to a pillar, which he hugs desperately.]

Hales: No.

Rebel 3: Come on, Hobb. It's your turn now.

Hales: No!

Farringdon: Come on!

Hales: Let go!

[**Farringdon** tries to prise **Hales'** fingers away from the pillar — unsuccessfully.]

Rebel 3: Got a grip on him!

Hales: Let go!

[**Farringdon** taps **Hales'** fingers with his sword-handle.]

Hales: N O ! !

[They drag him to the platform. He struggles so vehemently, it takes four of them to hold him down. **Sterling** sits on his legs and looks away. **Farringdon** swings and severs the head in one blow.]

Rebel 2: Neat job.

Farringdon: About time.

[He holds the head up and puts it on a pole.]

Farringdon: Let's jóin the others.

[They move across to join **Richard** and the other **Rebels**, who have now reached Mile End. He sees the heads.]

Richard: Good people, I am your King.

Rebel 4: Welcome, Lord King Richard. We'll have no King but you.

Richard: What is it you want? Tell me.

Farringdon: We want your permission to take and deal with all traitors.

Straw: No man shall be a serf, but shall give fourpence a year for an acre of land!

Rebel 2: No action shall be taken against us for what we've done!

Rebel 1: The Statute repealed and all offenders released!

Richard: Anything else?

Tyler: All this in writing.

Richard: I agree to everything. On condition you stop burning and killing and return to your homes. If you do this, I will set thirty clerks to draw up charters under the Great Seal, declaring that all men shall be free, and that you and your heirs shall be released for ever from the yoke of servitude and villeinage. I shall take no fine for the sealing and transcription. I also give my consent that you shall take all traitors, and I will deal with them by due process of law. Take this banner. It will show you act on my behalf.

[Cheers and applause as he hands over the banner.]

Come with me now and I will give you banners for Essex, Sussex, Bedford, Cambridge, Yarmouth, wherever you come from, and have your charters of freedom drawn up also.

Rebel 4: Long live King Richard and The True Commons!

[Cheers. **Richard** turns and goes off, followed by several **Rebels.**]

Farringdon: This list of traitors is now the law!

Horn: Those who wish to complain of any civil injury done to them within the walls of London, I and my followers will give you justice.

[They go.]

Rebel 1: We can get the Flemmies now.

Rebel 3: When'd they hurt you?

Rebel 1: Take all the jobs, don't they? Can't go near a draper's for the smell of Flemmies wafting out.

Rebel 3: Bollocks. We got what we came for. I'm going home.

Rebel 1: What's the matter with you?

Rebel 3: I'm tired, I've had a skinful and I miss my kids.

Rebel 1: Just one Flemmie, eh?

Rebel 3: I haven't had a poke for a fortnight.

[They go off. **Tyler** and **Straw** are alone.]

Straw: Well Wat, we've done it.

Tyler: The King's granting charters of freedom to the counties, that's all. Bits of paper. We may now legally take traitors, but due process of law will decide what happens to them. What does that mean? What the left hand gives, the right takes away again. We've got to keep this pressure up, define more closely what we want, make sure it happens. Otherwise we could lose all this as quickly as it's been won.

Straw: A lot of them are going home, Wat. There's all kinds of private, petty squabbles going on. We're not conquerors.

Tyler: You can't borrow power. As long as they're allowing us small measures of it, we haven't taken it. There's a long way to go yet.

Straw: You're cracking up. Your friend Lyons is on the list. I thought you wanted to get him while this lasted.

Tyler: I do.

Straw: Let's go and find the bastard then.

[They go off. On the balcony **Richard, Walworth** and **Sir Robert Knolles,** in heavy armour, appear. **Someone** announces:]

15th June: Carter Lane

Walworth: They've not kept their word, your Majesty. The violence has continued. Last night 150 Flemings were killed in the streets of London. John Legge was murdered and Wat Tyler is said to have killed Richard Lyons with his own hands. You can't bargain with these people. They've got no sense of diplomacy, of business.

Richard: I gave them my word, Mr Walworth.

Walworth: Your word can be repealed. It was forced from you. There's no shame in that.

Richard: I met them as they asked. I agreed to their demands. Many of them are happy with that and have gone home.

Walworth: They want to meet you again, your Majesty. They say the freedoms granted them yesterday aren't enough. They have more specific demands to press and they want these made law. It's not just freedom they want, they want to govern their own lives.

Richard: I can't punish all of them, just because a few cause trouble.

Walworth: The few are their leaders. They'll have us in the palms of their hands. We've seen what their leadership means: violence and anarchy. Many of your loyal merchants and knights who saw this rebellion at first as a protest against inherited privilege and Church domination and remained neutral, now see it as purely destructive. They stand to lose everything they've worked for all their lives. Their sympathy is with us. My good friend here, Sir Robert Knolles, has agreed to place his army at our disposal. Other loyal friends will do the same. We must seize our opportunity.

Richard: I understand your fear, Mr Walworth and I share it. But we shan't know what their leadership means until we see its face. In their terms those dear friends of mine they murdered were traitors. At the same time they've always called themselves my friends. Both sides will be in the dark until both declare themselves. Perhaps when we see their leader's face, and know how he behaves, it may be possible to deal with him. I've come to trust very much in your advice and support, Mr Walworth.

Walworth: Meet them tomorrow then, as they ask. A large open space somewhere outside the city would be best.

[Pause.]

Walworth: Say Smithfield.

[Pause.]

Richard: Well, Smithfield is a large open space outside the city.

Walworth: Thank-you, sir.

Richard: For what? I've said nothing.

67

Walworth: Sir?

Richard: I think we should go and pray for a good end to the day's proceedings.

[He goes.]

Knolles: What does that mean?

[Tight-lipped, **Walworth** follows **Richard.** This time **Knolles** is the last off. **Someone** announces:]

15th June: Smithfield

[The lights dim slightly. **Someone** sings the song, 'The Lion':]

The Lion is wonderfully strong
And full of wicked skill
And whether he play
Or seize his prey
He cannot choose but kill.

[**The Commons** come on with banners and one horse.]

Commoner 1: What we here for anyway?

Commoner 2: I thought it was all settled yesterday.

Commoner 3: Let's go home. We got what we came for.

Tyler: What we've got so far is nothing. They may say we're free; but as long as we need them to tell us so, as long as lords behave like lords and until every church and manor in England belongs by law to The Commons, they'll still hold power over us and still use us. That's why we asked for another meeting.

[**Richard, Walworth, Bramber, Philpot** and **Standish** come on with horses. They take up position opposite **The Commons.**]

Commoner 2: There he is, look!

[**Richard** takes **Bramber** to one side and whispers in his ear. **Bramber** crosses to **The Commons.**]

Bramber: Who is your chieftain?

[No answer. No movement.]

Bramber: Who will speak for you?

[Same. Pause.]

Commoner 1: We have no chieftain.

Bramber: Hurry. The King's waiting.

68

Tyler: You hurry, he's your lord. I'll come when I'm good and ready.

[**Bramber** returns.]

Tyler: He's there, we're here. They keep their distance and it's left to us to bridge it. We're supposed to be equals today, but is that a way for friends to meet? If I make a sign, go straight for them.

Commoner 2: Not the King, though. He's too precious. We can take him all over England with us and no-one will challenge us.

Tyler: [To **Commoner 3.**] You come with me. Stick close.

[**Tyler** spurs **The Commons' horse** over to **Richard,** close, so their horses' heads touch. He holds out his hand. **Richard** hesitates, then shakes it.]

Tyler: You see all those people?

[**Richard** nods.]

Tyler: Every one of 'em's sworn to do just as I say.

Richard: You're their leader, aren't you.

Tyler: They won't go away less we get what we want.

Richard: You shall have what you want.

Tyler: In that case, cheer up. In the next fortnight we'll be twice as much for you, and we'll be good mates.

Richard: Why won't you go home? If you break up now and go home, charters will be brought to each village in turn, as I promised.

Tyler: Hell boy, we're not going home with vague promises. If you don't keep that lot happy, they'll have the heads off these rag-dolls of yours.

[He gestures towards **The Lords.**]

Richard: If you tell me what you want, I'll have it drawn up under my seal.

Tyler: That's better. Now listen carefully. This must be exact.

[**Richard** motions **Philpot** to note the following down.]

Tyler: First: no law save Winchester law. The same civil rights for all. No justices and commissioners, but people shall arm and maintain peace themselves within their own districts.
Second: no more outlawry. All men shall be equally protected by the law until tried and found guilty by their peers.
Third: no lords shall have lordship in future, except the King, but it shall be divided up amongst all men according to their needs.

69

Fourth: no more Church privilege. There shall be only one Bishop, and all goods of the Church shall be divided up according to the needs of each parish, with provision for the reasonable sustenance of the existing clergy.

Fifth: no more serfdom. All men shall be free and of one condition.

That's it.

[**Philpot** finishes writing.]

Richard: All that you have asked for I promise, providing it is consistent with the regality of my crown. Now perhaps you could go home.

Tyler: Let's drink on it. [He grins at **The Lords**.] Something I can rinse my mouth on?

[Hesitation. **Bramber** offers him an ornate flask. **Wat Tyler** inspects its luxury, sniffs it.]

Tyler: That's the stuff. [He rinses his mouth, gargles, then spits it out in front of the King's horse, which starts. **Tyler** grabs its bridle.] Steady.

[**The Lords** bristle. **Tyler** grins.]

Tyler: Now. Something stronger? [He gives **Bramber** back the flask. **Walworth** hands him a flagon of ale. **Tyler** drinks noisily, offers it to the others. No response. **Walworth** takes the flagon back.] That's it then. We're equals. [He holds out his hand for **Richard** to shake. **Richard** shakes it. **Tyler** makes to ride off.]

Standish: Wat Tyler, I know you. You're the biggest thief and robber in all Kent.

[Pause. **Tyler** shakes his head in disbelief. **The Lords** encircle him. **Tyler** stays near **Richard**.]

Tyler: Still with us, are you?

[Pause. **Standish's** cloak is back, revealing his sword.]

Tyler: I'll have that knife.

Standish: That is the King's sword. Your hand is unworthy to touch it. You're a common thief.

Walworth: Take your hat off in the King's presence.

Bramber: You dare to mount your horse in front of the King?

Richard: Give him the sword.

[Reluctantly **Bramber** takes **Standish's** sword and gives it to **Tyler,** who throws it from hand to hand.]

70

Tyler: Now. Come here and say that.

[Pause.]

Tyler: Come on!

[Pause. **Standish** looks at the others. They agree and walk forward with him, a yard behind him.]

Tyler: [To **Commoner 3.**] In the name of King Richard and The True Commons, Will, have his head off.

Standish: On what grounds? I've said the truth. If the King weren't here, you wouldn't talk like that. [To **Commoner 3.**] Lay a finger on me and I'll kill you.

[**Tyler** moves round to defend **Commoner 3. The Lords** close in and separate **Tyler** from **Richard. Tyler** advances on **Standish. Walworth** blocks his path.]

Walworth: Now now, Wat, you can't do that.

Tyler: If I don't have his head, I'll not eat meat after.

Walworth: You can't talk like that in front of your King, Wat.

Tyler: Out of it!

Walworth: You're under arrest!

Tyler: Bollocks!

[He goes to stab **Walworth,** but the Mayor has armour. All **The Lords** pull back their cloaks revealing armour. **Walworth** strikes **Tyler** on the shoulder and knocks him from his horse.]

Commoner 2: What they doing?

Commoner 1: They're knighting him.

[**Bramber** and **Philpot** leap in and plunge their swords into **Tyler. Walworth** puts the boot in. **Commoner 3** backs off.]

Commoner 2: They're fucking not!

[**The Commons** put arrows in their bows. **Tyler,** on the ground, raises his sword.]

Tyler: Where are you?!

[The sword is kicked out of his hand. **Commoner 3** goes. **Richard** moves away from this melee towards **The Commons.**]

Walworth: Your Majesty!

Richard: No-one follow me!

[**Richard** rides over to **The Commons.** They are ready to shoot.]

Richard: What's the matter? Be still. I'm your King, aren't I? Come with me to Clerkenwell and you shall have what you ask.

[**The Commons** relax their bows. **Richard** turns his back on them and walks to **The Lords.**]

Commoner 1: Keep the King here. Organise.
Commoner 2: Wat's dead, though.
Commoner 3: Who's in charge?
Commoner 2: The King.
Commoner 1: No. Keep the King here. Organise.

[Etcetera. **Richard** reaches **The Lords. Walworth** and **Standish** go off, taking **Tyler's** body. **Bramber** and **Philpot** follow **Richard** to 'Clerkenwell', where **The Commons** go too. **Someone** sings the song, 'The Bear':]

Beware of the bear lest by chance he bite
He rarely stops play but to bite or smite.

[**Walworth** appears in the gallery.]

Walworth: Good people of London, go to St John of Clerkenwell's Fields. Your King is in danger, as are we all. Whatever you think of me, save your King. He needs your help.

[Immediately **Sir Robert Knolles** comes on, heavily armoured, with **Soldiers. Richard** and his **two Lords** see them and form an arc on one side of **The Commons. Knolles and Co.** move swiftly to complete a circle around **The Commons. The Commons** drop their bows and kneel.]

Knolles: Cut your bow strings.

[**The Commons** do so.]

Knolles: We ought to kill the lot of them now.
Richard: [stepping forward] Some are here against their will. We can't kill the innocent with the guilty. There'll be time for justice later. I'll have my banners back, though.
Knolles: Your Majesty.

[He collects the banners from **The Commons. Walworth** comes back with **Tyler's** head on a pole. He kneels.]

Walworth: Your Majesty.

[**Richard** stares at **Tyler's** head. **Bramber** and **Philpot** kneel too. **Richard** goes over and knights them.]

Richard: Rise, Sir Nicholas Bramber.
Rise, Sir John Philpot.

Walworth: Your Majesty, I'm a merchant, I live by trade. I'm neither worthy nor able to support a knight's estate.

Richard: I'm much indebted to you, William Walworth. A hundred pounds in land goes with this knighthood.

[**Walworth** swiftly drops to his knees.]

Richard: Rise, Sir William Walworth.

[They all turn to look at **The Commons. Knolles** finishes collecting the banners, which he brings to **Richard. Richard** takes one of the charters and reads:]

Richard: 'Richard, King of England, to all his bailiffs and faithful men, greetings. Know that by our special grace we have manumitted from serfdom all our subjects of the counties of Essex, Kent, Hertford, Bedford, Suffolk, Norfolk and Cambridge. And we have pardoned our said subjects for all felonies, acts of treason and transgressions performed by them in whatsoever way. We also withdraw sentences of outlawry against them because of these offences. And we hereby grant our complete freedom to each of them.' This is your charter, witnessed by myself in London on the 15th June in the fourth year of my reign. Now go home.

[**The Commons** go. **Richard** folds the charter up and smiles. **The Lords** go.]

Richard: Thank God. Today I recovered my heritage and the realm of England, which I nearly lost.

[Immediately **Someone** announces:]

Jack Straw, John Sterling, Alan Threader and other rebel leaders were sought out and executed the same night as Smithfield. Three days later Richard the Second issued the following proclamation to his sheriffs and constables: 'Because various of our subjects have risen in various counties against our peace, affirming that these risings were done with our will and authority, we hereby notify you that these risings displease us immensely and are a source of shame to us. Wherefore we command that our subjects desist completely from such assemblies and return home in peace, under penalty of losing life and limb and all their goods.' The rebellion spread as far North as Peterborough and as far East as Yarmouth. In St Alban's the rebel leader William Grindcobbe wrung a moderate charter of freedom

from the local abbey. In Bury St. Edmunds the rebel leader
John Wrawe killed the local abbott and Lord Cavendish,
at that time Chief Justice of England, and made their heads
kiss in the market square. In Cambridge the Mayor and town
rose and burned all records of university privilege in the
market square. By this time a certain Bishop Henry de
Spencer had taken it upon himself to put down the rebellion.
The flying Bishop Spencer and Robert Tresilian, the new
Chief Justice, rode down through East Anglia from
Peterborough, subduing the uprisings one by one. The usual
method of trying rebels was to pardon whole vills if they
testified against their leaders. Thomas Baker, who started
the uprising at Brentwood, was hanged at St Albans, as were
William Grindcobbe and John Ball, who was disembowelled
while still half-alive, and the four quarters of his body
posted around the city as a warning. Middle-class leaders
like Thomas Farringdon and Alderman Horn generally
escaped with only blemished reputations. By the end of June
Richard the Second had got the hang of the game and was
riding through Kent and Essex conducting the repression
personally.

The last real opposition to fall to Richard, Justice Tresilian
and The Flying Bishop was in Norwich, at that time the
second city in England. It was led by a local dyer called
Geoffrey Lister, who was proclaimed 'King of the True
Commons', and having organised and enlisted the
co-operation of many of the local knights and landowners,
he was conducting a difficult social experiment:

21st June: Norwich

[**Geoffrey Lister,** in dyer's clothes, comes in with **Adam
Clymme,** a messenger. **Lord William de Morley** fans them
with a large fan.]

Lister: The whole of Norfolk answers to us now, Adam. Our sheep
and our fishing have always made us the richest county in
England, and yet our people always felt hard done by.
They did all the work and London got all the profits.
Now, if we see people all right, more and more come over
to us. Even knights and lords. This is Lord William de
Morley by the way.

Morley: How do you do.

Clymme: Fine thanks.

[**Morley** goes on fanning.]

74

Lister: What's your news?

Clymme: The Bishop's taken back Cambridge and Tresilian's hanging everybody. They'll be in Suffolk soon. That means John Wrawe'll be in trouble.

Lister: The King's made the grown-up's league after all.

[**Lord John de Brewes** comes in with food. **Lord Stephen de Hales** follows.]

Lister: Food. You hungry?

Clymme: I've ridden forty miles today.

[He goes to take some food.]

Lister: Hang on.

Clymme: What's the matter?

[**Lord Hales** tastes the food.]

Lister: This is Lord Stephen de Hales. My taster.

[**Clymme** is amused.]

Lister: I had to give them something to do. It's a good lesson in being equal. It lets people know you mean what you say.

Hales: All right.

[**Clymme** goes to eat. **Lister** holds him back.]

Lister: Give him a minute. It's a completely different country up here, Adam. We're financially independent. I'm even thinking we might bargain with London.

[**Two Peasants** come in holding down **Sir Robert de Salle,** who struggles against them. **Lister** jumps up.]

Lister: What's the idea?

Peasant 1: Sir Robert de Salle, Geoffrey. He wants to speak to you.

Lister: It's all right, Sir Robert. We don't mean to hurt you if you're good.

[**The Peasants** let go of **de Salle.**]

Salle: I refuse to collaborate in any way.

Lister: Why? These men have. They're as good as you.

[**Sir Roger Bacon** comes in.]

Salle: Not on the field of battle, sir.

Lister: We've all done our bit. [He sees **Sir Roger Bacon.**] Sir Roger! [They embrace.] Good to see you!

Salle: Why have you joined these men, Sir Roger? You're a brave knight and a noble soldier. These men are debasing our

rank. Look at this! [**Hales, Brewes, Morley.**] Slaves! They're
bribing and bullying our class to its knees.

Bacon: We're fighting for people, Sir Robert. Not titles.

Salle: Do you call these people? [He includes **The Peasants.**]

Peasant 2: Shut up! [He shoves **Salle** roughly.]

Lister: For your own sake, Sir Robert, be careful. We're of like
mind here. We respect your courage and energy as a knight,
but you started life as a workman, the same as me. I'm a
dyer, your father was a mason. You could be a great help
to us. You know our people, they'll accept what you say.
We're not out to debase you, but to raise them. A leader of
ordinary people must be their servant or power can run away
with him. If you join us, a quarter of England will be under
your command.

Salle: Under the command of treachery! I'd rather be hanged!
As you will be certainly!

Peasant 2: I'll kill him!

[**Peasant 2** rushes **Salle.**]

Lister: No!

[**Salle** turns to defend himself. As he draws his sword,
Peasant 1 rushes to help **Peasant 2. Salle** slips. **The Peasants**
fall on him. **Peasant 1** cuts his throat. They look up, uneasy.
Silence.]

Lister: [angry] Take him outside and wait for me!

[**The Peasants** carry **Salle** off.]

Lister: Sir Roger, this is Adam Clymme. He's been riding as a
messenger for the rebels in East Anglia. Sit down, please.
Sir Roger took Yarmouth yesterday, Adam. — How's it
going?

Bacon: Very well. We've broken the guild stranglehold on Yarmouth
Market and I've put my men in charge of the Customs.
That's why I've come. I've got some money for the fund.

[He gives it to **Lister.**]

Lister: We've got this fund, Adam. If the local nobs pay us a fee,
we assume they're friendly and there's no need to take action
against them. It's our own exchequer. I thought we might
give the King some. Try and win him over while we're still
strong. I'd like you to take two of my gentlemen and ride
down to London. We want a charter of manumission and
royal approval like the people at Smithfield got. I've drawn

up a draught. [He hands it to **Clymme.**]

Lister: Give that and the fund to the King. If we can get to him
before the Bishop and Justice Tresilian, we may still buy
the right to live as we were born to. I'll show you the horses.

[They go off. **The Actor** who sang 'Man beware' at the
beginning comes on and sings it again:]

Man beware and don't hold back
Think upon the block and on the axe
The axe was sharp, the block was hard
In the fourth year of King Richard.

[**Two Peasants** come on and begin building a gallows,
though this is not immediately obvious.
Someone announces:]

28th June: Billericay

[**Richard** comes on. He recites 'The Dragon'.]

Richard: I shall swallow you humans, regardless, the lot,
Yet some I might spare — others not.

[**Justice Tresilian** and **Bishop Henry de Spencer,** who wears a
helmet, two-handed sword and chain-mail over his cassock
which is hoisted to his knees, come on.]

Richard: I've got a very good army, haven't I, Justice Robert.
Tresilian: Very good, sir.
Richard: Cousin John will be surprised when he gets back from
Scotland. There's hardly been any resistance at all, has
there, Bishop Henry.
Bishop: They're unarmed, unskilled and undisciplined. With 500
trained men we've scattered ten times that number today.
Richard: We shan't have any more trouble in Essex, shall we.
Bishop: Your Majesty, with respect, there'll always be isolated
groups. Though sooner or later they'll succumb. Certainly,
as a concerted movement, they're finished.
Tresilian: Those we don't finish in battle, we'll hang.
Richard: We can't kill the entire male population of East Anglia,
Justice Robert. There'd be no-one left to farm the land and
care for our wool. I think the time has come for mercy.

[**Brewes** and **Morley** come on.]

Brewes: [kneeling] Your Majesty, we've been sent on a commission
from the rebel leader Geoffrey Lister. He offers you this
money to show his good faith and requests you grant him a
charter of manumission, the details of which he has drawn

up on this paper.

[He holds the paper out. **Richard** takes it but continues to hold out his hand. **Brewes** gives him the money. **Richard** tears the paper up. He feels the weight of the money in his hand.]

Richard: I might get the crown jewels back with this.

Brewes: We've ridden in company with three of the rebels, your Majesty. They were surprised to find you so far North.

Richard: Bring them here. Along with the prisoners taken today.

Brewes: Your Majesty.

[**Brewes** and **Morley** go off.]

Richard: Now gentlemen, are we ready?

[**Tresilian** finds a table to hold court at. **The Bishop** takes off his helmet.]

Richard: I think the time's come to tell them.

[**The Prisoners** come in, escorted by **Brewes** and **Morley**. They stand in a line.]

Richard: Do you wish to say anything on your own behalf?

Prisoner 1: We want confirmation of the charters of manumission of serfdom granted by your Majesty to the commons of England.

Richard: We have revoked those charters, and you are all traitors against our kingdom. But we will not be unkind. If you hand over to Justice Tresilian those who have been your leaders, the rest of you may go home in peace, and you will hear my answer.

Prisoner 2: Sir, behold him here by whom this town was first moved.

[**A Prisoner** is pushed forward. It is the same actor that played **Thomas Baker** in the Brentwood scene. **The Peasants** have finished the gallows. It goes up.]

Richard: Miserable and detested men, who have sought to be your lords' equals, you are not worthy to live. You were and are serfs, and you will remain in bondage not as before, but incomparably viler. For as long as we live, we shall do our utmost with all faculties at our disposal to suppress you, so that the rigour of your servitude will serve as an example to posterity. Both now and in the future people like yourselves will always have your misery before their eyes like a mirror, so that you will be cursed by them and they will fear to do as you have done.

— Richard the Second at Billericay, 28th of June, 1381.

For a list of books and pamphlets available
write to:

Pluto Press

Unit 10, Spencer Court,
7 Chalcot Road
London NW1 8LH
telephone 01-722 0141

Steve Gooch is actively involved in community theatre. He has written two other plays published by Pluto Press, Female Transport and The Motor Show.

Steve Gooch

Female Transport

Six working-class women have been convicted of petty crimes in early nineteenth-century London. *Female Transport* is a tough and realistic account of their six month voyage to Australia, locked together in a ship's cell.

From their tentative and desperate first steps in coming to terms with each other and the oppression of their all-male jailers, to their final disembarkation as a tight-knit bunch of hardened rebels at Sydney, the play shows what effects decisions made above deck produce on the 'cargo' below.

'Charts the growing spirit of resistance and self-awareness among six particular women as they come to recognize clearly where their strength lies.'
Naseem Khan, *Time Out*.

Steve Gooch and Paul Thompson

The Motor Show

'The Motor Show' is an account of sixty years of struggle by the working class and their trade unions against the Ford Motor Company. The Motor Show uses songs and a fast succession of music hall, documentary and realistic scenes to show the history of the Ford Empire; from the Model T and the introduction of the production line, through the slump of the 1930s and the war, to the industrial relations struggles of recent years.

The Motor Show was first performed in Dagenham to an audience of carworkers and their families. It was later transferred to the Half Moon Theatre, London.